MW01064851

DANGER CITY

urban short fiction

2005

contemporary press

This is a work of fiction. All of the characters and events portrayed in this book are either products of the authors' twisted imaginations or are used ficticiously.

DANGER CITY – urban short fiction 2005

Copyright© 2005

All rights reserved, including the right to reproduce this book, or portions thereof, in any form.

Cover Design by Chris Reese

A Contemporary Press Book
Published by Contemporary Press
Brooklyn, New York

Distributed by Publishers Group West
www.pgw.com

www.contemporarypress.com

ISBN 0-9744614-8-2

First edition: April 2005

Printed in the United States of America

Liner Notes

Late in 2002, Contemporary Press was born on a typical, drunken evening in New York City. In addition to publisher/writer Jay Brida, the other members in attendance at that first meeting were writer/editors Jess Dukes, Jeffrey Dinsmore, and Mike Segretto, and designers Dennis Hayes, Jennifer Lilya, and Chris Reese.

The job market was for shit, and we were all tired of having to smoke corporate cock to make a buck. None of us had yet written our great American novels, so, with the courage only a happy hour beer can provide, we took matters into our own hands. The following week, we all threw in a few hundred bucks and started Contemporary Press.

And we're glad we rolled those dice, because now we're an LLC, we've had our egos stroked in national, glossy magazines, and we're distributed throughout North America by the very cool Publishers Group West. Even though we all still have our day jobs, Contemporary Press is our passion. By the end of 2005, we will have published 10 books, and we have no other plans but to keep rolling out our sexy, crazy pulp novels for years to come. Shit, we even have an accountant. Yet with all our good fortune, we're careful to stick with what we know--and that's why we still conduct the majority of our business every Wednesday night over drinks at our favorite local bar.

The book you hold in your hands, *Danger City*, is a proud achievement for us. Culled entirely from open submissions, the stories come from mostly unpublished authors who we think really deserve a shot. We started this company with the intention of publishing not just our own writing, but other great and unknown writers who know the value of an entertaining story and don't feel like kissing miles of ass to get their stuff published.

We appreciate the support, and we hope you enjoy *Danger City*.

Cheers,

Contemporary Press

Mike Welch – In Search of Johnny Three-Legs

It was a real important dinner. Real important. Really. All of the important people were there, Dinsmore, Brida, Perez, Blue Ellis, Mortensen, Ski, Jim, mom, dad, the crew from Contemporary Press, and unfortunately, Rory Carmichael. I was having the time of my life when that prick Rory jumped up on the table and ruined everything. Thanks for saving the night Blue.

Todd Robinson – Delivery

For the Robinson, Giglio, Shaker, Rezendes, and McGlinchey families. For my family with whom I don't share names or blood, who believe more than I do sometimes.

Jeffrey Kuczmarski – Max Find

Jeffrey Kuczmarski pins the rap for Max Find on the following suspects: April "Blind Mole" Krukowski, Eric "Three Fingers" Canafax, Dusty "The Weasel" Traum, Mark "The Walleye" Steinmetz, Phyllis "Mimosa" Moore, Kyoko "Knitting Needle" Mori and all of his other fallen angels.

Vinnie Penn – Diary of a Superhero
Vinnie Penn is a writer/radio personality/comedian/occasionally decent human being from New Haven CT. After years spent free-lancing as a music writer for magazines like Hit Parader and Circus, and then doing his own radio morning show since 1997, Penn is giving novels, screenplays, and selling crack a shot.

Sean Beaudoin – Jakes
Sean Beaudoin lives in San Francisco with his daughter Stella, who prefers Richard Scarey.

Jon Michael McCarron – Namith's Mission
Jon Michael McCarron is an actor and writer born and raised in Clio, Michigan. Please don't hold that against him. Schooled on the hard streets of East Lansing he has seen and done more than anyone has a right to. And yes, he does validate. Jon wishes to thank his awesome parents Roger and Linda, his grandparents Jackie and Orville and his brother Joe, all of whom continue to offer him unconditional love, support, and food.

Carl Moore – Empire of One
Thanks to Sarah for digging imagination, friends and family for letting me speak in tongues, and franchises everywhere for dystopias that are delicious and fun to eat.

Mike Segretto – We All Scream for Ice Cream
Mike Segretto is the author of the novels Dead Dog, How to Smash Everyone to Pieces and the upcoming *The Bride of Trash*. Mike would like to thank his friends, his family, and his personal Guru, the Enlightened Bahattamatma Mavatinashishoo.

Dana Fredsti – A Man's Gotta Eat What a Man's Gotta Eat
To Mom, Bill, and Chris who put up with hours of zombie movies; Brian, who bought me most of 'em and watched 'em with me; Lisa, for much writing encouragement; Dad, who told me I write like a misogynistic middle-aged drunk man; Maureen, a swell dame if ever there was one; and Dave, for all the MT moments.

Jeff Somers – Ringing the Changes
Under laboratory conditions I have nurtured my own ego into a huge, healthy beast with rippling muscles and thick, downy hair. But I have also entrusted servants with Elephant Guns to blow its brains out if it ever slips its chains and starts hurling feces around the place.

Roman Bojanski – The Kilt
Roman Bojanski splits his time between Chicago and Miami. He has worn a mustache since the age of 13, and this is his first published short story. He thanks the good people at Contemporary Press.

Jeffrey Dinsmore – Faggy on the Streets
Jeffrey Dinsmore wrote his first novel for CP, Johnny Astronaut, under the pseudonym Rory Carmichael. His second CP novel, I, An Actress, will be coming out under his own name. He thanks everyone in his life but especially baby Lexi.

Mike Cipra – Loving the Monster
Despite rumors to the contrary, no lizards were harmed during the research for this piece. The author is indebted to T.C. Boyle for his help editing the story and to all the remaining wild creatures in the world—you know who you are—for your love and inspiration and yes, even your venom. Let it flow.

CONTENTS

In Search of
Johnny Three-Legs

by MIKE WELCH

My office was on the corner of Western and Wilshire Boulevard in the Wiltern Building. The rent was cheap and the little office was conveniently hot in the summer, freezing in the winter. So I had that going for me. It was decorated pretty much how you'd expect a private investigator's office to be decorated, or at least I liked to think so. I'd been fascinated with the occupation since I was a kid and not much has changed since then except I wear bigger shoes and I've got a shit load of alimony and child support to pay. I was sitting in my chair with my feet up on my desk, because that's how we private investigators sit when we're waiting for that sexy broad to walk through the door and dump a heap of their troubles in our laps. We promise to sort their problems out for a hundred and fifty bucks an hour and a few glimpses of thigh and cleavage. The only trouble was, no sexy broads had walked through my door since I started my business a year ago. In one year, I've only handled two insurance frauds and a cheating wife case. The insurance frauds were boring work and the cheating wife was my own, Kathleen.

So I had my feet up and my chair tilted back just to the point of toppling over. I was staring out the window, fifteen floors up, wondering what it would be like to jump from fifteen floors up. I knew what the result would be. 'But how would the fall feel?' is what I really wanted to know, as I tilted my chair back a little bit further. Then a little bit further and BOOM! I was on my ass. I knew it would happen, but I couldn't help myself. I lay there for a moment picturing myself on the pavement below. Then I tried to get up but couldn't. The space was too cramped behind my desk to maneuver properly and it took some struggling just to get untangled from the chair. That's when she walked in, the sexy broad. Just what I'd been waiting for my whole life, a childhood fantasy come true and I was flailing around on my back like an overturned turtle.

"Hello?" she said, not sure if anyone was in the office.

I sprang up.

"Hey."

"Is everything alright?" she asked.

She was unbelievably sexy. She was wearing a snug sweater, three buttons undone from the top, mini-skirt and knee-high boots. Yes, everything was all right.

"How can I help you Miss ...?" I said, coolly, with my hand out. She stared at it like it was a diseased rat.

I motioned for her to sit down as I wrestled my chair up off the floor. I grabbed a pack of Kents out of my top drawer and offered her one. She accepted and I searched for a lighter. Top drawer? No. Second drawer, no. Bottom drawer, no. I smelled smoke. I looked up from my desk. She had her cigarette lit and was holding a Zippo in my direction. I nodded, lit my cigarette, and together we smoked. I inhaled, she exhaled, I exhaled, and she inhaled. It was sexy.

"Is this a business call or a social visit?" I asked, realizing a little too late it was a corny thing to ask. I reminded myself again to be cool.

"What do you think, Mr. Douglas?"

"I think you should tell me what it is I can do for you."

"I need you to help me find Johnny Three-Legs."

"Was he a boyfriend, husband ...?"

"A dog."

"Yeah, most men are." I said with a laugh. She cut me short.

"A dog Mr. Douglas, you know, ruff ruff."

I cocked a skeptical brow.

"You want me to find a dog?"

"Yes," she answered.

"Well," I said, leaning back in my chair, feet up on the desk, "perhaps you should call on a pet detective for your situation."

She smiled. It was a crazy but beautiful smile.

She stubbed out her cigarette and looked me straight in the eye with that crazy smile frozen to her icy cool stare.

"Perhaps I should knock your fucking teeth through the back of your head?" She cooed.

She had my attention.

"What kind of dog are we looking for here, Miss ...?" I asked, again searching for a name.

"We're looking for a three-legged dog."

She reached into her fashionable leather bag and pulled out what looked like a furry stick. She set it on my desk.

"This belongs to Johnny Three-Legs. Find the rest of him."

I picked up the stuffed leg. She gave it to me as if it were a color swatch for some rare fabric.

"How'd he lose it?" I asked, staring at the dog leg.

"In an act of heroism. He is a great dog. When the vet couldn't re-attach his leg, I took it to a taxidermist. Johnny Three loves to sleep with it."

"Where was the last place you saw Johnny Three-Legs?"

"In my front yard. I live in Beverly Hills on Rodeo Drive."

"I'll find your dog, Miss ... Miss ...?" she ignored me. "I'll find your dog, but I'm going to have to charge you my missing person rate," I told her, while twirling the dog leg.

"That's fine, just find him as fast as you can," she said, as she stood up.

Her breasts were at eye level, so I stared at them.

"Mr. Douglas, try not to be so obvious. If you want something from me," she said looking down at her breasts then back at me, "then find my dog."

She took my hand and wrote a phone number and her name, Barbara, on it, then turned for the door.

"Uh, hold on ..."

"Yes?" She purred.

I wanted to ask for my retainer fee but I was too stupid with lust.

"How'd you know my name?"

"Mr. Douglas, try not to be as dumb as you are obvious," she advised, and as she shut my door behind her I could see my name, Rex Douglas, Private Investigator, on the door, just as I'd always wanted.

I leaned back in my chair with my feet still firmly planted on the desk and wondered aloud, "Where am I gonna find this three-legged dog?" Then I leaned back a little further, and a little ... BOOM!

***

I'd left the top down on the convertible. The car seats were blistering hot from the morning Los Angeles sun. My back was sweaty and sticking to the fake leather. The gas gauge was bouncing on empty and some heartless bastard stole my stereo, so I sang to myself, "R-O-C-K in the USA, yeah rockin' in the USA." I cruised up and down the palm tree-lined streets of Beverly Hills slowly, searching each yard and every inch of sidewalk for Johnny Three-Legs. Camden, Rodeo, Rexford, then Palm. From a pedestrian point of view I must have looked like I was casing the multi-million dollar homes for a big score and, to tell you the truth, part of me wished I was.

After covering the better half of the neighborhood, I decided to try a different tactic and turned down Fairfax toward the Thirsty Liver. Chances of the dog being in a bar were slim, but it was worth a shot, and the chances of a shot being in a bar were strong.

My eyes took awhile to adjust to the darkness of the bar, and when they did, I wished they hadn't. The Thirsty Liver was an ugly place. Good old Ed and Jim sat at the corner of the bar and I sad-dled up next to them. Ed and Jim were permanent fixtures in the joint. I admired their lack of ambition. It made their lives seem so much easier. Joe was tending bar.

"What's up, Joe?"

"Not much Rex, what're ya havin?" he asked with a grin.

"A bad morning, rotten luck with the ladies, and intermittent diarrhea."

"I got just the thing."

He poured me a tall glass of Jameson over ice with a Budweiser back.

"Thanks, Joe."

I clinked glasses with Ed and Jim, then drank the whiskey down and followed it with a hefty pull from the Budweiser. Ed was the first to say something.

"How's it hangin', Rex?"

I just stared at my beer. Ed and Jim were nice guys but horri-ble bores.

"Yeah, me too," Jim said. Whether he was being sarcastic or responding to something that hadn't been said was anybody's guess.

Ed and Jim were always living vicariously through other bar regulars. I usually had some wild story for them but today I just didn't feel it.

"I'm lookin' for a dog named Johnny Three-Legs," I said, mostly to myself.

"Any leads?" Ed asked, holding on to the bar with both hands.

"Nothin'."

"Shit," Jim said.

"Shit's right," Ed said.

"Shit a gold monkey," Joe said, for reasons unknown down at the other end of the bar.

It got quiet.

"I suppose he's only got three legs?" Jim asked, as if he couldn't help himself.

"No, he's hung like a buffalo," I replied, sarcastically.

"How'd he lose his leg?" Ed asked, now that the conversation door was open.

"An act of heroism." I replied, and hoped they would leave it at that. They did.

"Shit," Ed said.

"Shit's right," Jim agreed.

"Motherfuckin' shit," Joe said loudly from the other end of the bar into the receiver of the phone.

I finished my beer and motioned to Joe for another one. He gave me the 'hold on' finger and pointed to the receiver against his ear. I gave him the 'take your time' wave.

"What's that you're foolin' with?" Ed asked.

"The fourth leg."

"Can I see it?" Jim asked.

I flipped it over to him.

"The woman who lost her dog gave it to me, thought it might help me find him."

"A woman huh?" Ed wondered.

"Yep."

"She pretty?" Ed had to know. He and Jim always had to know about the women.

"Very."

"Big tits?"

"C'mon now Ed, it's a business thing. How in the hell would I know?"

Ed hung his head a little. For stupid guys, Ed and Jim were pretty sensitive.

"Yeah Ed, she has big tits."

Ed smiled and took a big swig of his beer. I looked over at Jim and he was scratching the dog leg.

"Jim, what in the fuck are you doing?"

"You think he can feel this?" Jim asked, seriously.

"Who?"

"The dog. The dog that lost it," Jim said, excited.

"Give me the leg, Jim."

Jim handed the leg back to me. Joe brought me over a beer and we drank in silence. I looked at the number on my hand. I downed my beer, and another, then another.

***

I had intended to only have a couple of beers and then continue my search but the day got away from me. Ed ordered a round of shots and we toasted.

"Here's to this stuffed leg and the dog who it belongs to, wherever he may be. May we find him in good health," Ed toasted sincerely holding up the stuffed leg.

We touched glasses and drank.

"Whose good health, ours or the dog's?" Jim asked.

"Both," Ed appeased.

Then I ordered a round and it was my turn to toast.

"Here's to cruel women and spoiled rotten kids."

Ed and I poured our drinks down our throats while Jim just sat and stared at me.

"Why would we drink to that?" Jim asked.

"I was being sarcastic, Jim. Feeling a little sorry for myself, I guess."

"We have to do that again. I'm not drinking to that."

Jim ordered another round for Ed and I. We lifted our glasses in the air while Jim thought of a toast.

"A three-legged dog walked into a bar," Jim said.

"Well that's a joke, Jim, not a toast. I liked Rex's better," Ed said in my defense.

Jim pointed over my shoulder towards the door.

"No, a three-legged dog just walked into the bar."

I spun on my stool and there he was, sniffing around the doorway. I grabbed the leg off of the bar, crouched down and gave a whistle.

"C'mere, boy."

The dog hobbled over to me. I let him sniff my hand, then gave him a firm scratching between his ears. I held the leg up to see if the colors matched and they matched perfectly. He gave it a sniff and started wagging his tail and licking the leg. I didn't know if he recognized it as his leg or if it was the hot wing sauce Jim got on it earlier in the day. I looked at the number on my hand and reached for my cell phone.

***

Johnny Three-Legs seemed to be enjoying his ride in the car. He was hanging his head in the breeze, tongue flapping in the wind, dog spit flying all over the side of my car. He would bark at passing cars then look at me for approval. I gave him a nod and a thumbs-up once, but I had other things on my mind.

The woman seemed shocked on the other end of the phone that I had found her dog so quickly. I admit I got lucky but I wanted to use this little miracle to my advantage. I hadn't been with a woman since Kathleen and I had a feeling if I played my cards right, I might be able to extend the good-luck streak.

We pulled up to the Beverly Hills address she gave me. It was one of the smaller houses on the street but still large as far as houses go. It was a contemporary house, not what I imagined her in, but I could still see myself seducing her in her bedroom. My palms started to get sweaty.

I walked around to Johnny Three-Legs' side of the car.

"C'mon boy." I said, giving my thigh a couple of pats. "C'mon, let's go see mama."

He jumped out of the car, sticking close to my side as we followed the path up to her door.

I rang the bell and the beautiful woman from my office answered.

The woman looked down at Johnny Three-Legs then back at me.

She was stunning. I felt a stir in my pants. Then I realized Johnny Three-Legs had the cuff and was pulling me back towards the car.

"There you are, sweetie-pie," she said to the dog. I imagined she was saying it to me.

Johnny Three-Legs didn't give her the time of day. She reached down cautiously to pet him and he let go of my pant leg just long enough to snap at her. She jumped.

"Whoa, he must be confused. I'm sure he had a rough few days," I said, trying to make the situation a little less uncomfortable.

"Why don't you come in, Mr. Douglas?"

"Thanks," I said, as I slipped past her, dragging her three-legged dog behind me. Something strange was going on but I had one thing on my mind. Two, really, and the only thing between them and me was one tiny, cashmere sweater.

"Thank you so much for finding my little baby," she said, a bit nervously.

"It was no problem at all. Really, my specialty is missing people, so finding a dog was no problem."

"Well, let me write you a check."

She walked over to the bar and looked through her purse.

"Oh dear, my checkbook isn't here. It must be in the bedroom," she said, and headed towards the hall. She didn't get too far before stopping and turning to me. "Would you like to come with me, Mr. Douglas?"

Without saying a word, I walked toward her. Dragging Johnny 3 along.

"Uh, could you leave the dog behind?"

I tried to free myself from him, but he wasn't having any of it. I remembered his fourth leg and took it from my pocket.

"Here you go, boy," I said, as I tossed it down to him.

He let go of my pants, took his leg and went to lie by the front door. I followed Barbara to the bedroom.

***

She turned her back to me and took off her sweater. Then she reached behind her back and unhooked her bra. She slipped out of her jeans with one swift movement. She turned back around to face me, then shimmied out of her thong underwear. Just as I suspected, there was no checkbook in the bedroom. She wanted me. Sometimes I even surprised myself with how perceptive I can be. I stepped closer and in an instant she was on me. Our mouths locked and I realized just how long it had been since I touched a woman.

She dragged me over to the bed and tugged my pants down. I threw myself down on her and as she struggled for a comfortable position on the bed, I entered her.

"Ok ... slow ... slow it down a bit ... just ..." she whispered but I couldn't hear her because;

"OOOOOHH YEAHHHHH!!!"

As fast as it started, it was over. I lay there on top of her like an out-of-shape wrestler, panting, sweaty and more than a little self-conscious. I could hear Johnny Three-Legs whining in the other room.

"Ok, big boy," she grunted, as she pushed me off of her.

"You want a drink?" she asked me, as she put on her robe.

"No thanks," I panted.

"I think you're going to need one," she told me, and walked out of the room.

I didn't like her tone and I was kind of wondering what happened to the post-coital cuddling. What about the after-glow?

From the other room, I heard what sounded like the voice of another woman.

I wiped myself off with her sheet, pulled up my pants and went to see what was going on.

Barbara was arguing with another woman who had her back to me. Johnny Three-Legs was hog-tied to the dining room table.

"This should have been over with by now," Barbara yelled in a hushed tone. "Gustavo is going to be pissed off."

"I can't do it, he's too damn cute," I heard the woman whisper.

When Johnny Three-Legs saw me, he tried to yelp, but his little snout was wrapped in duct tape.

"What the fuck?" I asked, because I wanted to know what the fuck.

The woman spun around. It was my ex-wife Kathleen.

"What are you doing here?" I asked. She looked strung out.

"Hello, Rex," she said with tiny icicles dangling from her voice.

"What the hell are you doing with Johnny Three-Legs?" I asked as I stepped between the women and Johnny Three-Legs.

"Well, your bitch ex-wife was supposed to have him split open so we could get our heroin. But you came too quick and she chickened out," Barbara ranted.

"You're the one who lost the dog in the first place," Kathleen came back.

"Well, excuse me for trying to do something nice for you. I stopped on the way home from the airport to pick you up a *grande* half-decaf soy latte so you'd stop complaining that it's just sex between us. I try and do something nice and everything's my fault," Barbara shrieked.

"You could have picked a better time to be nice than on your way home with a dog full of heroin," Kathleen pointed out.

"You ungrateful bitch," Barbara said as she slapped Kathleen across the face.

Kathleen reared back and connected her fist to Barbara's forehead. Barbara dropped like a bag of cement. Kathleen turned to me. She picked up the huge carving knife that was intended for Johnny Three.

"Kathleen, let's be reasonable here," I pleaded.

"Do it, Rex. Cut open Johnny Three-Legs and I'll split the money with you after we deliver the heroin to Gustavo."

"You can rip a man's heart out but you can't cut open a dog?"

She looked at me for a second.

"That's real sweet, Rex. Step aside, I'll do it."

"No," I yelled, "I'll do it for you."

I grabbed the knife and stepped to the table. She stood close behind me and watched.

"Do it right. Don't cut too deep or you'll split open the capsules, and if they mix with blood, they won't be worth a shit. That's what Gustavo told us."

"Who the fuck is Gustavo?" I asked.

"He's the man," she replied, as if I should have known.

I held the knife with both hands and lifted it above Johnny Three's belly. But first I needed to know something.

"Why'd you leave me for Barbara?" I asked, hoping she'd say something I might understand.

She paused.

"I needed some excitement Rex—the white picket fence, the Sunday paper, watching you floss every night, it was boring the shit out of me. Barbara knows how to live. She gets the best drugs, parties all night, sleeps all day. We travel."

I couldn't hear anymore. This wasn't my wife talking. I stared at her, trying to see what I saw ten years ago when we first met. But there was nothing left. The sparkle in her eye was gone, deadened by the best drugs Barbara could buy.

I lifted the knife again. I took one hand off the handle and with a smooth fist pumping motion I brought my elbow squarely into

Kathleen's stomach. She doubled over instantly. I grabbed her by the hair and smashed her face against the table. She fell to the floor. A river of blood ran from her nose. She coughed and spit out a tooth. I cut the restraints off of Johnny Three-Legs and we got the hell out of there.

***

When I got in the car I made two phone calls: one to Joe the bartender, to see if he really 'knew' people and the other to my friend Phil the veterinarian.

"Hey Phil, I know it's late, but can you meet me at your office? It's an emergency. My dog has a really bad stomach ache. I'll make it worth your while."

After a couple of hours with our pal Phil, Johnny Three-Legs and I made our way to the Thirsty Liver. By the time we got there Joe had made good on his word. A well-dressed man sat in the darkest corner of the bar. I walked in carrying a paper sack full of heroin with the freshly stitched up Johnny Three at my side.

"Is that the guy, Joe?" I whispered.

Joe nodded and continued to clean beer mugs. I walked to the table.

"You got it?" I asked, as I approached.

"Got it," the well-dressed man answered.

"You got it?" he asked me.

I handed over my sack of heroin. He looked inside. He handed me a box. I looked inside. I smiled and went to the bar. I saddled up next to Ed and Jim.

"Drinks on me, Joe," I told him, and I meant it this time.

***

After closing time, Johnny Three-Legs and I spilled out of the bar and hopped in the convertible. We were about as happy as two drunks could be. I had never seen a dog drink beer like that before. I breathed in the fresh night air as I drove past my office knowing I'd never step foot inside there again. But what I didn't know was where we were going as I passed up my street and jumped on the interstate, both of our heads hanging out the window, barking at the passing cars.

Delivery

by TODD ROBINSON

"I got Northern Lights, Grape Ape, Kryptonite, Silk, White Rhino, White Widow, Emerald Gold, Bubble Gum, and Double Bubble," Jamie said to the skinny doe-eyed girl leaning on the doorjamb of her apartment.

She bit her lip nodding, mulling over her options. "Don't you have any more of that Kush I got last week?"

"Was Kush in that long list I just recited?"

The girl blinked, confused by the question. "I don't remember."

Jamie gritted his teeth. "It wasn't." *Goddamn potheads*, he thought. Their short-term memory was more often than not blown to the four winds anyhow. Hell, his own wasn't much better. Even though his patience was getting shorter with the girl, Jamie appreciated the reprieve from the chill fall rain outside. But Christ, time was money here.

"Oh. I liked that one. Real mellow smoke." The girl nodded into her statement, like a pecking bird.

"Might have some next week."

"Got any G-13?"

Despite the fact that Jamie hadn't included the pharmaceutical grade strain in his list, he always carried two packets, in case. He just didn't think that this girl, answering the door in her beat-up Berkeley sweatshirt, had the scratch to buy the stuff. It was the most top-notch weed ever produced. *Thank you Uncle Sam*. "Yeah. It's a hundred-fifty."

"Whoa."

He knew it. He'd delivered to this girl four times in the past month and had never sold her anything better than Kryptonite or Kush, neither of them being too expensive. She acted like he was one of the Fenway hustlers who sold teenagers baggies cut with oregano. He only sold weed rated from really good up to G-13, but the girl obviously had no idea what the hell she was talking about. "Try the Silk. The high is pretty close."

"To the G-13?" Her eyes widened in hope.

"No, to Kush. Nothing is close to G-13. If there was, you couldn't afford it."

"Screw you, I can afford it."

Jamie was tired of the exchange. He wanted to make the sale and get out of there. He didn't need to get into an argument with the twit about her budget. "Listen, you buying today, or not?"

"Give me the Silk."

"Fifty." Jamie reached into his pocket and drew out the small bag. The girl handed him a rolled-up mess of singles and fives. She held her hand out impatiently.

"Wait," Jamie ordered as he unfolded the bills and counted. The girl sighed with annoyance. Jamie would have chucked the money in her face and walked if Hugh wouldn't have chewed him out for blowing a sale.

"Fifty even." *Thank God*, Jamie thought as he slapped the bud into her hand. She made no effort to close the door gently.

Bitch.

***

Jamie waited at Model Bar for his next call, sipping a Heineken. Most days, he didn't mind riding his bike. Some guys had bought themselves scooters or dirt bikes to motor around in. Jamie still liked riding his bicycle. It was slower than anything motored, but not by much. On his bike, he could still choose which traffic laws to obey, which lights to run, and any route he wanted. The guys on motors had to be double careful not to catch the cops' attention. That was one thing Jamie was good at. On the street, he was the Flash, the Invisible Man, and Keyser Soze all rolled into one. You think he's there and poof ... gone.

Except in the rain. And it was cold. Summer rain wasn't so bad, could even be refreshing. But this crap was for the birds—ducks, specifically. So, he sat there like a wet dog, alone in an empty bar. The snooty bartender was arguing on her phone with somebody.

Then his cell phone rang.

"Yeah"

"Twenty-two Cabot Street, Roxbury."

"Dammit, Hugh. Don't be sending me to Roxbury in this weather." Jaimie thought, *Don't send me to Roxbury at all*, but didn't say it. The day could have been sunshine and kittens. Roxbury was still a hell run.

"Bring the G-13."

"What? Aw, hell no. Have you looked outside?"

"Apartment 2-E." Click. Hugh didn't argue, much less with his employees. You made the delivery, or you returned to the base, handed over your stash, and never returned.

It was most likely the rain that kept Roxbury safe. On decent days, every corner had a crew of hoods on it. They weren't necessarily Crips or Bloods, but those guys were out there, too; mostly, dealing themselves, sometimes looking for the next sucker to jack. All of them were dangerous, but they tended to deal exclusively on the high end of the drug spectrum. They peddled crack, horse, coke. Ecstasy was blowing up big time in the suburbs, but designer drugs stayed with the designer people, living in their designer homes and clothes.

Jamie was aware of his place. Yeah, he was a scumbag drug dealer, but he was positive nobody ever OD'ed on what he sold. *Gateway drug, my ass.* Jamie smoked weed regularly since he was old enough to roll, and he never felt the urge to upgrade his drugs.

Yeah, Jamie knew his place. Knew the game, and he didn't like rolling dice in Roxbury. He got jumped once on the lip of Roxbury. That night, some gang-bangers recognized him from return trips and mugged him. Only they weren't content with a simple robbery. Jamie spent three weeks hospitalized, a month before he could get on a bike again. Hugh, offering the thug's health plan, covered Jamie's hospital costs. The lost merchandise and money came out of Jamie's pocket, though.

When Hugh visited him, his condolences were, "Watch your back next time."

Jamie had his reasons for not responding. One, his back wouldn't have mattered. They'd swarmed him from all sides. Two, his jaw was wired.

***

On the outside, 22 Cabot wasn't a bad building for the hood. The inside was another matter. The checkered floor looked like it hadn't been washed in years, and Lord, the smell. A part of it was cooking odors. There was a pleasant air of spice underneath the rest of it. What remained on top made his stomach churn: wet decay mixed with a piss.

Jamie pinched his nose as he walked up the stairwell. Somebody was yelling in Russian. Another had their television turned way loud. Alex Trebek said, "Montecello."

Who the hell would be living in this dump and buying G-13? Maybe the person who called was going to rob him, knowing he would be carrying the best stuff. He had no choice, though. Make the delivery or be out of a job. He wished for a weapon. Some of the other guys carried a piece. But Jamie didn't want to take the chance of getting searched. He didn't need weapons possession added to the charges he would already be carrying in his backpack. Besides, he knew his capabilities. Jamie wasn't a brawler, but he could run, given the right reasons, and once he was on his bike, he was gone.

Two-E. Jamie knocked. He heard rustling inside and a deadbolt click. The door opened a crack, and a small Hispanic woman peeked out. "Can I help you?" she asked softly. Her voice was tinged with an accent. What Jamie could see was pretty as hell. The eye in the crack was a deep brown, long lashes.

For a second, Jamie forgot what he was there for. "Uh, yeah. Delivery?"

"You bring pizza?" She peeked a little further and looked at Jamie's empty hands.

"Uh ..." This had never happened before. Somebody screw up their delivery numbers? "No, I ..."

"Jen! Who you talkin' to?" A male voice yelled behind her.

"Is a delivery," she replied.

Jen fell away from the door, pulled roughly back. "The fuck you doin' answering the door?"

Aw no ... He knew the voice. Trezza.

21

Trezza swung the door wide. He was shirtless, muscles twitching at Jamie. He'd grown a gut, but he was still huge. And all things equal, he was most likely a sociopath, too. Through the door, Jamie could see the apartment. Considering the building and the neighborhood, the apartment was relatively nice.

"S'up?" said Trezza. "You one of Hugh's boys?"

"Yeah," Jamie lied. Thank God for small favors. Trezza didn't recognize him. Not that there was any beef, but Jamie preferred anonymity where Pete Trezza was concerned. Jamie delivered to Trezza a couple times, years ago. He would've been happy to never have to again.

"What you got?"

"I got Northern Lights …"

Trezza grabbed him and pushed him hard into the wall. "I'm talkin' G-13, bitch. You think I can't afford the good shit? Save the skunk for the sororities, bitch."

Jamie's legs went weak, remembering what Trezza had done to Ike. "Yeah. I got two packets." He tried to keep the fear out of his voice, but felt it trembling, anyway. Self-loathing flooded through Jamie. His nerves told him to run; his pride said "fight back." The brain won. Fighting back would be suicide, or at least more hospital time. Jamie wasn't eager for either.

Trezza smiled. "You scared, Pee-Wee?" Jamie didn't respond. Trezza knew that he was. "You should be. You know what happened to the last guy tried to rip me off."

Jamie nodded.

Trezza let him go. "Damn, only got two? I got my boys coming over. Two packets ain't gonna do it."

"I only got two."

"What's the next best?"

"Depends. Kryptonite and Silk are both …"

"Gimme it all." Trezza waved his hand and pulled a wad of hundreds from his pocket.

When Jamie went to his pack, he saw around Trezza's legs. Jen sat on the couch. She and Jamie locked eyes for a moment. Well, locked eye was more appropriate. Her left eye, the one that Jamie couldn't see in the crack was swollen shut. The biggest part of her was her stomach. She was very, very pregnant.

"What?" The sharpness of Trezza's tone snapped Jamie back. Again, he had no response. Trezza's gaze hardened as he looked back and realized. A backhand clipped Jamie across the face, lightly, but enough to humiliate him. "Mind your own."

Jamie noticed tracks in the crook of Trezza's elbow.

***

"I can't believe you sent me there." Jamie was pissed. Hugh knew Trezza's history. Not only was Trezza one of the biggest heroin dealers in Boston, but a year ago, he beat down another delivery guy. Jamie was pissed, not only that they were still delivering to the prick, but that Hugh sent *him*.

Adding to that aggravation was Jamie's difficulty finding Hugh's new place. Hugh kept his operation mobile, since four armed guys hit his place in Brighton. It was righteous paranoia, but he'd forgotten to tell Jamie where he moved. Jamie had to ride an extra hour in the rain while he tried to connect with Hugh to bitch at him.

"Trezza's a customer." Hugh didn't lookup from his scale, as he carefully weighed out the packets.

"Ike ..."

"Ike ripped him off. And, he was ripping me off."

Ike made himself some extra cash by selling fake G-13. Trezza knew the difference and took it out on Ike. That was over a year ago. Ike was still eating through straws. "He threatened me."

"How much did he buy?" That was going to be the checkmate. Louder than words, the money would trump any argument. "Six hundred," Jamie mumbled.

"How much?" Hugh asked again, holding his hand against his ear for emphasis.

"Six hundred," Jamie yelled.

"'Nuff said." Hugh pinched off a small portion of pot from an enormous bag and placed it on the scale.

Jamie tried once more. "Looked like he's hitting his own goods."

"Don't care."

***

Jamie rode for as long as he could; trying to push his frustrations out with each pump of the pedals. The anger just moved through his body as he shot through traffic. It was getting dark before Jamie headed home to Southie. He let himself in through the basement door, rather than track filthy rain over his mother's rugs. The last thing he needed was a hissy fit from his mother about not being able to have nice things. Nice things being the ten-dollar Oriental rug runner purchased twenty years ago from K-Mart.

"Jamie? That you?" His mother called down the stairwell. Jamie peeled off the wet clothes that stuck to him like Saran Wrap.

"No, Ma. It's a psycho, here to steal your Hummels."

"Don't be a smart-ass." When his mother was aggravated, her Southie accent deepened. Jamie could tell she was in a state when she called him 'smaht-ass.'

"What now, Ma?"

"Your dinner's almost cold."

"Yell at me when it's cold, then." It was Thursday: shepherd's pie night in the McGowan house. It wasn't very good, even when it was hot. Jamie's mother suffered from the culinary challenges that faced generations of Boston's Irish.

Jamie heard her mutter another "smaht-ass" as she shuffled off. At the least, living in the basement afforded him some privacy. His mother's bad hip left her paranoid about tumbling down the stairs.

Jamie's mood didn't leave him room for much of an appetite, anyway. Instead, he rolled himself a small joint. That would help his attitude and give him enough munchies to eat the cold shepherd's pie.

For a few weeks, he suffered mild paranoia when his phone rang. His gut clenched between answering and getting the address. He dreaded having to go back to Trezza's. After some time passed, so did his worries.

***

Four months later, Jamie was at the Model, like always, waiting on the next delivery. His phone chimed on the bar. His stomach flip-flopped and he almost knocked over his Heineken.

"Twenty-two Cabot Street, Roxbury."

"Aw, hell no, Hugh ...?" Jamie didn't want to whine, but he heard his voice squeak, anyway.

"Twenty-two Cabot Street, Roxbury."

"C'mon, can't you ...?" Jamie cut the complaint short. Somewhere irrational, he hoped that it was another apartment. There was more than one in that shit hole.

"Apartment 2-E." The phone disconnected.

The old anger and fear washed over him when he walked out the door. Jamie threw his phone down onto the concrete. The plastic shattered, and Jamie felt a small release. At least Hugh would have to buy him a new phone. *That'll teach the prick to send me to Trezza's again.*

Jamie rode as fast as he could to the address and ran up the stairs. The whole ride across town, Jamie convinced himself that it was better this way, facing his fears, and all. *Hell, who am I kidding. I'm scared shitless.*

He smelled it from the other end of the hallway. At first, Jamie thought it must have been coming from somewhere else. The smell of diapers and pizza (that was all he could identify) was definitely coming from apartment 2-E. A quick edit of slasher films projected through Jamie's imagination.

The door opened wide this time. Jamie couldn't see anyone inside. Then he looked down. A kid, no older than five, stood there, smiling. His Spongebob pajamas looked as though they hadn't been washed in weeks. Jamie remembered Jen and her eye. The kid looked just like her, but the nose was Trezza's. Trezza had the type of nose that had obviously taken a few pops here and there. So had the kid's. Jamie tried not to think too hard on it. It only brought back hardcore memories of his own father and his eager willingness to lash out. Jamie had scars on the back of his legs. Staring at the baby's disfigured nose made the old marks burn as if the leather had just whipped across. He smoldered with an anger he'd thought long dead when the kid took Jamie's fingers and led him inside.

"Is your Daddy home?" Jamie felt like an asshole for even asking. In the months since Jamie had been there, the apartment had gone to hell. The kid pulled Jamie to the coffee table and opened a

Cohiba box. For a second, Jamie thought the kid was offering him a cigar. He wasn't. Inside was an unopened hypodermic, matches, spoon, and a packet of heroin. Jesus, the kid was offering him a hit. He'd probably seen Trezza do it so many times that he'd adopted the gesture.

"Uh, no thanks," Jamie said through numb lips. *From watching you, Dad. I learned it from watching you.* Jamie remembered the old anti-drug campaign and would have laughed if he wasn't so horrified.

A toilet flushed and out walked Trezza. He stopped, wide-eyed, when he saw Jamie. He charged him like an enraged bull. Trezza looked like hell. He'd dropped at least thirty pounds, which only meant that he outweighed Jamie by about fifty. He grabbed Jamie and drove him into the wall, knocking the wind out of him.

"The fuck you doing in my house? The fuck you doing with my box?" he screamed. Trezza's eyes were wild, darting all over Jamie.

"Nothing," Jamie wheezed, his lungs spasming.

"Who the fuck are you?" Trezza reached into his back pocket and pulled a gravity knife. He pressed the tip to Jamie's throat. "Answer me!" Again, Trezza failed to recognize Jamie. This time, Jamie wished he did.

"Dee ... delivery," Jamie stuttered hoarsely. *Don't let me pee. Please don't let me pee.*

"Asshole." Trezza bashed Jamie on the nose. Blood gushed from his nostrils as he crumpled to the floor. "Don't ever let me see you in my house again." He turned to the kid. "And what the fuck are you doing?"

The kid was crying, pleading to Trezza in panicked Spanish. Jamie didn't understand anything the kid was saying except for "Papi."

Trezza slapped the kid brutally. The kid wailed, terrified and hurt.

"Quit it!" Trezza hit him again, harder. The kid balled up, his cries drawn into whimpers.

Trezza rifled Jamie's bag, looking at the packets. Taking what he wanted, he threw the backpack at Jamie, lifted him by the shirt, and tossed him out the door. Peeling off some bills, he tossed the cash at Jamie's feet and slammed the door. Jamie then heard more yelling in Spanish—Trezza's voice, harsh and abusive. Jen's pleading. Jamie heard flesh smacking and more sobbing. Then an infant's weak cries joined the din. Jamie half-crawled, half-fell down the stairs as he fought to escape as fast as he could manage.

***

"Jamie, please ... what's wrong?" Jamie's mother hovered at the top of the stairs. She heard Jamie when he came in; probably because when he did, he lost control and threw his bike across the room. It landed with a crash that could probably be heard downtown. His mother started crying when she heard the tears in Jamie's voice.

"Leave me alone, Ma!" Jamie couldn't stop crying. His nose wouldn't stop bleeding. It wouldn't stop. None of it would stop.

"Please, Jamie," she sobbed. "I can't help you. I can't come down there."

"Just go away, please." Jamie curled up on the musty carpet. Everything hurt.

Then his mother said, "I miss your Dad, too."

Jamie let her think that.

***

"You get the license number?" Hugh gave him the once over as Jamie held ice against his swollen nose. Hugh, with his usual style, expressed slightly more sympathy than a brick.

Jamie shook his head. He would have said "no," but he was trying to avoid any words using the letter N. The sound sent bolts of pain into Jamie's sinuses. "Guy bumped me and jetted." The excuse worked for two reasons since Jamie didn't have to explain the busted phone.

"Doesn't look like you need stitches." Hugh was looking at the cut on the back of Jamie's head. Jamie guessed that he'd suffered it while tumbling down the stairs. He heard Hugh sigh with relief. Probably less in concern over Jamie than at the decreasing possibility that he'd have to foot another hospital bill. "You sure you don't want to get checked out? You might have internal injuries."

Jamie shook his head carefully to keep his nose from leaking again. "I fell od my head." Jeez, talking was difficult.

Hugh sighed. "Good. I mean ..."

Jamie waved off Hugh's apology. "Weh he calls, I wah Durah's delibbery."

"Huh?"

Jamie repeated himself, as best he could.

Hugh shrugged. "I'm not understanding you."

"Durah!"

"Terror? What terror?"

Jamie grabbed a notebook off the desk. There was no way to say it without *N*'s. He wrote on the paper: "When he calls, I want Trezza's delivery."

Hugh read the note and smiled. "You two kiss and make up?"

Jamie shrugged. "Good tipper."

***

It was raining again when Jamie went back to Cabot Street. Jamie's sneakers squished wetly on the stairs. The rank smell was worse this time. It had been three months since Trezza broke Jamie's nose. It healed badly, leaving him with a lump on the bridge and unable to smell through his left nostril. The closer he got to 2-E, the more he wished that neither one was operational. Before he got to the door, Jamie opened his backpack and put the baggie in his pocket. He didn't know if the opportunity would arise, but he'd waited three months for this.

He knocked.

Nothing.

He knocked harder. Jamie's heart picked up the pace; not from fear, but from wanting, from anticipation.

"Get the fuggin' door," came a slurred voice from the other side. Jen opened the door a crack. She wouldn't look into Jamie's eyes.

"Delivery," was all he said, flat-voiced.

Jen opened the door wider and walked back towards the kitchen. No bruises Jamie could see, but she had a pronounced limp.

"'Bout time," said Trezza from the couch. He looked like he'd dropped another thirty pounds. The once intimidating frame looked like someone had made a scarecrow out of the discarded remains of an anemic.

Jamie fought off the violent rush he felt course through him. For once he had the upper hand. Jamie remained calm.

"Gimme the weed," Trezza snarled.

Jamie walked over and placed the packet onto the table, next to the cigar box.

With difficulty, Trezza drew a significantly smaller wad of sweaty cash from his pocket. Trezza stared at his hand like he wondered how it got there.

"How much?" Trezza drooled onto his lips and wiped it away with his forearm. The tracks made a connect-the-dots game, mapping out the veins on his arm. "Fifty for what's there."

"Sheesus. Fifty bucks for pencil shavings," he muttered. Trezza slapped the bills into Jamie's palm.

Jamie needed to buy some time. "Can I use your phone?"

"The hell for?"

"Battery died on my cell. I gotta call Hugh."

"Whatever floats your log."

Jamie picked up the phone and dialed.

"... at the tone, the exact time will ...."

"Yeah, Hugh. It's me."

"... beeeeeeeeeeeeeeeep ..."

Trezza stood and stumbled to the bathroom. Jamie hung up and opened the cigar box. He pulled the baggie from his pocket and compared. There was more in his bag, but he doubted that Trezza would notice or care. If there was less, Jamie had no doubt that hell would have broken loose on Trezza's family. The color was right. Jamie added a few dashes of cinnamon to the Clorox before bagging it. He placed his bag into the box.

The toilet flushed and Jamie dropped the heroin on the floor. It landed next to a tiny foot in a SpiderMan sock. He bent quickly to pick it up and saw the kid under the coffee table. The boy put a finger to his lips. He didn't want Jamie to give away his hideout. Jamie winked as he palmed the drugs. Then he held his own finger to his lips, smiling. The kid grinned and put his hand over his mouth to stifle the giggles.

Jamie was gone before Trezza made it back from the bathroom.

Max Find

by JEFFREY KUCZMARSKI

The sun was bright and terrible on my face so I took a healthy swig of whiskey before I fully opened my eyes. I had fallen asleep at my desk. My head pounded like a bass drum, and the air was too healthy to breathe on its own, so I lit a smoke. The phone rang evenly, like a call to prayer.

"Max Find here," I said with a touch of syrup in my voice. I needed the money.

"Mr. Find, our son, Tommy, is missing."

"Yeah, what about it?"

"Well, you are an investigator—"

"Yeah, lady, but I don't do missing children. Call the police."

"We'll pay you two thousand in cash," she said desperately.

"Okay, be here in an hour," I said, hanging up the receiver.

I didn't bother to clean up the office. I did take another swig of whiskey, splash cold water on my face and make a pot of black tar no one would recognize as coffee.

***

Mrs. Janet Parker was a doll. She had on a black skirt and had long red fingernails that sunk into a man from fifteen feet away. She wasn't high class but she wasn't a plain-Jane either. She certainly wasn't anybody's mommy. She looked dangerous. My heart beat triple time in my chest, but that was probably just the tar in my lungs stealing bases.

"So, what's the deal, Mrs. Parker?"

"My son's been missing for three weeks now. Haven't seen him since New Year's Day."

I asked all the usual questions. "Your son a drinker? Does he visit prostitutes? Is he a drug runner? Has he been locked up recently?" The sweet smile on her painted lips evaporated and her face reddened enough to make her beautiful.

"What are you implying? That my son is some sort of criminal?"

"Yes, that's right, Momma. It's been my experience that people don't just disappear. There's usually some reason. Maybe he pissed off the wrong guy by looking too long at his lady? Mothers usually don't come to a guy like me. They call the police. Have you called the police?"

"Yes. The cops don't care for a little guy like Tommy."

"What's the racket?"

"It's a delicate matter. Tommy's been roughed up before but he's never disappeared. Will you look into it?" she asked, waving four unwrinkled Franklins in my face.

"You're not his mother, though, are you? You're too young and too good-looking. Stop lying." I said, flattering her.

"Why, thank you," she said, batting her eyelashes and showing off her thighs. "The men at the warehouse where he works were always picking on him, calling him Dummy. I drop him off and pick him up. I know my son. It's not like him to wander off. Are you going to help me or not?" She purred so sincerely that the varnish on my desk started to peel.

"Yeah, I'll do it."

I went over what I had so far about the case: Dummy's real name was Tommy Parker but no one called him Tommy.

"Got a name? Somewhere to start?"

"Talk to Bully Wentford."

***

I kicked Bully Wentford's front door with my left foot, hard enough to make the door rattle in its frame. A big slug of a man poked his sweaty face against the glass, puzzled. I gave the door another good kick and he opened the door a crack. There's nothing like hospitality to get someone's attention.

"Can I help you?" shrieked the fat slug.

"Yeah, you worked with Tommy Parker."

"I never heard of him," he said pulling the door closed.

I stuffed my size twelve in the shrinking crack and pushed hard on the door, hitting him in the face, which made a wet sound like soft butter hitting the floor. I let him know, "This can be easy or this can be hard, pal. I've got questions. They're not real tough. We'll start out with the easy ones." He started talking once I bounced his head off the wall. I like that in a slug.

"Okay, okay. What's your beef with Dummy?" asked the slug, rubbing his gigantic head.

"No beef, pal, Dummy's missing and I want some info. Okay?"

"Yeah sure."

"So, what do you know about him? You worked with him. Did you know him?"

"Sure, but it's not like I really ever talked to him. He was a freak. Christ, he tore a guy's face half off once for teasing him," he said, turning paler than sour cream. Seems even Dummy had an epiphany once in awhile.

"Did he have any enemies?"

"No, but he didn't have any friends either."

"Anything stick out in your mind, fatty?"

"Well, Leroy Bogs always came down on Dummy real hard."

***

Leroy Bogs was nobody's fool. He had greasy hair, a beer gut, and the dim eyes of a snake on a cold day to prove it. Leroy Bogs thought his shit smelled like a bouquet of yellow roses. He was wrong. Leroy played fast and hard with the truth, but I broke him of that habit with a pool cue over what passed for his cranium.

"Now, are you ready to play ball, big man, or should I find a thicker cue?" I asked into his oily, stinking face. "You ever saw a baseball game, Bogs? I used to pitch a little. Let me try one of these balls," I said, reaching for the eight ball. "Betcha it'd make a nice sound bashing in your teeth." It's amazing what happens when you bring dentistry into the picture.

"So, I heard you liked to pick on Tommy?"

"Yeah, but that's nothing. Everybody picked on Tommy."

"When was the last time you saw Tommy?"

"His dad picked him up right around New Year's. If I were you, I'd check out his folks. I heard his mother is a big roller."

"You got an address?"

"Hell no. You're the damn detective. Haven't you heard of a phone book?"

***

I left Bogs on the floor, still breathing, laying in the dirt and the muck and the slime where he belonged. Bogs was mean, but he was only a bully. He didn't seem to know anything more than the Slug. I probably should have started with Tommy's parents, but I'd learned a long time ago to explore my options. I harassed the phone book from the bartender and looked up Parker, called the operator, and got the address.

I stopped by my office first, and the phone rang like it always does when I have things to do.

"Find, here." It was Mrs. Parker. "Hey, doll-face."

"They found Tommy's body in the river. I want you to come over right away." She gave the same address as the one on the napkin in front of me.

fifty-one forty-five North Ventura Avenue was a yellow brick job with a screened-off front porch, built when they still used to build them that way. I leaned on the bell. Mrs. Parker came to the door, and I broke out in a sweat when she answered, taking my arm in hers.

"Now, that's not a very motherly thing to do."

"Isn't it?" she asked coyly. "Daddy's waiting in the sitting room," she motioned, leading me on.

Tommy's dad, Mr. Rudolph Parker, was a squat cigar-smoking man with a nose red enough to guide Santa's sleigh.

"So, Rudolph, where's your son?"

"Isn't that your job? We're paying you."

"For what exactly? Some sham investigation? I think I'm gonna give my pal at the cop shop an earful. My dialing finger is real itchy."

"Now wait a minute. I don't like what you're implying."

"I don't much like you either, Rudolph, so where does that

leave us? I want straight answers."

"Okay, okay. Tommy is not my son but he is Janet's. But my paternity has nothing to do with this."

"He's been bobbing for apples in the river. Why use me? Why not the cops?"

"I think Tommy saw something. He was upset. Said he couldn't sleep but he wouldn't say why. He was afraid. Someone was trying to keep him silent. After he disappeared, Janet heard about you and called," he said draining his glass and pouring another scotch.

"So, you took out a life insurance policy on him and then took him for a swim?"

"No, I loved Tommy like a son. We had no life insurance on him." Rudolph was looking like a fat, rich, drunk ... but not a killer.

"Now that you're done accusing us, let me show you the door," said Janet Parker with more ice in her voice than in Mr. Parker's glass

At the door, she whispered for me to meet her at the Emperor gambling boat.

***

I drove around the block and parked out of sight then waited for three hours. I was down to my last smoke when Janet walked out to her silver BMW in a little black number that didn't exactly qualify as a mourning dress. I tailed her at a safe distance down Lake Shore Drive and caught a glimpse of her as she boarded the boat. A couple of mugs at the door looked grim until I slipped them a couple of Grants.

Janet was at the black jack table with her arms around Frankie the Fish.

"Rudolph sleeping? Too drunk to guide your sleigh tonight? I hope you gave him a good-night kiss."

"Mr. Find, I didn't know you were a gambling man."

"I'm not. I don't like fish. If you can smell it, it's gone bad."

Frankie smirked. "Find, I haven't seen you for a while. Still playing private dick, eh? I could use a man of your talents here. Two fifty a day. No more nickel and dime work. What do ya say?"

"No thanks. I'm allergic to your kind. No, I rather like my nickel and dime work. What are you doing here, Mrs. Parker? Is this what Tommy saw? Did he see you sneak out every night in the arms of this two-bit thug?"

"She doesn't have to answer to nobody but me in my place, Find. Boys," he called, pointing to two goons with necks as thick as rolled carpets, "show Mr. Find the river."

I made a break for the door but my legs were kicked from under me and a fist came down on the back of my neck. Blackness swallowed me.

***

I awoke in the back seat of my car alive enough to appreciate the pain. Frankie's boys had done a nice job. I crawled into the front seat and drove to the office. The phone rang, and I put the receiver to my swollen face.

"Find."

"I'm sorry about last night."

"Me too, Mrs. Parker, me too. What's going on? I don't like being a punching bag."

"Meet me at noon at the Gin Mill and I'll explain."

***

The Gin Mill was filled with the usual lunchtime crowd, grabbing a quick fix before their afternoon drudgery. Mrs. Parker sat huddled in a booth near the door.

"Does it hurt terribly?"

"I've had worse. I know how you can make it better."

"Oh, I could make you forget, but now is not the time. Mr. Parker is dead."

"When? How? You're pretty bad luck. I didn't sign on for this."

"Yes, I guess I am bad luck," she said, tearing up. "I thought it was over. I never thought he'd find us."

"Who? Stop talking in riddles. Tell it plain."

"My other husband, Jack."

"How many do you have, lady?"

"A lady never tells. You must help me."

"Why should I? You've got the fish man. What do you want with me?"

"You're in the business of finding people. I want Jack found before something else happens to me."

"I'm not so sure you need my protection."

"Oh, but I do," she said more with her watery green eyes than her pretty little mouth.

"Why did your husband kill your son?"

"He's crazy. He never wanted children, so I ran off. I had Tommy anyway. Jack was jealous and hateful and not afraid to use his fists, so I ran to Chicago and started a new life. I met Rudy. Please help me. I don't know where else to turn."

***

I searched for Jack Mankowic for a week and a half, when I tracked him to a motel on the Upper West Side. I found a broken man on the verge of death.

"So, you're Jack?"

"How do you know my name? She sent you, didn't she?"

"Your wife?"

"Yes, I knew she would. Are you going to kill me now, put me out of my misery?"

"Why did you kill your own son?"

"Kill Tommy? Is that what she told you," he said and laughed bitterly. "I swear, it wasn't me," was all he got out before the door was kicked in by Frankie's goons and I was knocked cold.

***

I woke up strapped to a chair in the dark hull of a ship. Blood dripped from an open wound on my forehead, stinging my eyes. Unattended, I worked feverishly on the ropes that bound me until I was able to slip one hand free, then the other. I rose cautiously up the ladder and pushed the hatch gently open. One of Frankie's boys stood guarding the hallway with his back to me, smoking. I turned off his lights and grabbed his revolver, creeping forward down the hallway to Frankie's office, hoping no one heard the scuffle.

Another of Frankie's mutts stood guarding his office door. I put my finger to my lips with my gun leveled at his belly and motioned for him to open the door.

"Awake already? I knew I should have dumped you in the river when I had the chance." Janet sat, coolly smoking. She did not smile.

"Honeymoon's over already? Why did you do it?"

"Oh, Jack got me knocked up when we were kids, but I had a better life to live. I worked for Rudy, and he fell real hard real fast, so he agreed to take care of Tommy and me. I tried squeezing old

Rudy for more money, but he was too tight to give me anything but a taste. I figured if I married him, I could milk him for more, but that was taking too long, so I went to Frankie and asked him to make sure that the old limp bastard had an accident."

"And Tommy?"

"I got Tommy a job working for Frankie in the warehouse. He caught Frankie and me on all fours in the cafeteria one night and told Rudy. Rudy went through the roof and told me I was cut off and that Tommy was going to inherit everything. Tommy never could keep his mouth shut. He ran off to get away from me—hid with Jack. Stupid boy," she said, pulling a derringer from her purse. No one moved except me. I pulled the trigger of my borrowed snub-nosed revolver. I felt her bullet graze my shoulder and saw her body crumple to the floor like a flower in a hurricane. Before I walked out, I made Frankie clean up his mess, and then I taught him how to swim.

Diary of a Superhero

by VINNIE PENN

You think that we don't exist, but we do. You think that we're works of fiction, but we're not. We're real. We're here.

It happens one of two ways: Born with it, or freak accident. The unenlightened believe that to be redundant.

In any event, I am a case of the former; one in a long line of what we refer to as "flyers." My family has been here for generations. Some used their powers for good, some for evil, and some not at all. My father used to say, "Sometimes the only difference between the good guys and the bad guys is a cape."

He always made great observations like that, and I was fortunate enough to be on the receiving end of most of them. Mine simply get written out here, on the pages of a journal I got as a stocking stuffer one year from a girlfriend who obviously hadn't gotten to know me at all. I used the first few pages for love letters but when she suddenly moved out of state, leaving behind no forwarding address, I caved to her subtle suggestion that I make note of my thoughts. Mostly out of boredom.

Recently I lost my dad to the most nefarious nemesis of them all, old age. Unbelievable. A man who once carried an entire planet on his shoulders dying in his sleep.

June 4

Busy day today. Work was unexpectedly frantic and with this new boss constantly breathing down my neck using my ultra-speed is impossible. I swear I'm the only superhero whose alter ego puts in OT.

I was fully prepared to fly straight home from the office, especially with Sinisterio finally out of the picture, but, noooooo; two street thugs decide today's the day they're going to take a jewelry shop.

So, I'm soaring above Jameson Jewelry when I see these two idiots launch a brick through the window. I swoop down and discover another overtime victim directly in their path, albeit a much better looking one. The poor thing is petrified. One of the mutts grabs this hottie by her hair and starts leading her towards the vault.

Next thing I know there's a gun by her head and the threats are practically triggering the alarm she never activated in the first place. Fortunately, hyped up on caffeine and still hovering, I realize that if I land on the store's floor with enough oomph I can shake the place, and maybe them, too.

Well, overtime led to overkill and boom! I almost bounced the three of them up to the ceiling. Anyway, I subdued the two wannabes and kept the girl from danger, so everything was cool.

She was incredibly appreciative, too, and once the police whisked the would-be crooks away she blew me. That damsel-in-distress stuff doesn't usually work for me, either, but this chick was capital H-O-T and I was crazy horny.

June 10

Damned insomnia. People think we "patrol" the city streets out of social responsibility. Yeah right! You try sleeping with everything inside you working at ten times the normal rate. I've had to re-do the carpet in the hallway from my bedroom to the bathroom eight times in the last three years.

Nights like this, I wish I wasn't a natural born superhero, but one of those experiment-gone-awry types like Bullittproof. I gotta remember to mention this to him the next time we go for beers. He's always droning on about how he's gonna sue those bastards at the university. "Quarters of kind were selling real cheap. All I needed was a couple extra bucks. I wake up a hundred dollars richer and bullet proof. A man should be able to shoot himself with dignity, need be. Blah blah blah. Boo hoo."

Let's put things in perspective here, I tell him: He's got childhood memories, a grasp on what normal is at the very least, and he even had a say in his name (you can usually tell who does by the spelling).

I'm still annoyed they call me The Flying Avenger. How lacking in creativity is that anyway? I lobbied hard for The Flying Fist. Besides, Avenger's what they called my father and his father before him. Good Lord, technically I'm Flying Avenger III! That's better than Junior, sure, but still kinda non-threatening when confronting someone hell bent on taking over the world.

Can you picture some twisted bad guy yelling, "Flying Avenger the third, how did you find me!? By the way, how's your dad?"

Bullittproof had the luxury of deciding on a name before he even ventured out into the world of heroing. If I remember correctly, he did a bit of a media blitz at the time, too.

June 16

I've been thinking about the day my father told me I was a flyer. Damn Harry Chapin on the radio.

I had barely gotten my sea legs from walking, yet there he was throwing me off the roof of the garage.

"There are very few flyers left in the world," he beamed as we crept up to the peak. "You can do what others only dream about. And dream about constantly, I might add."

"Lose teeth?" I thought on my way down, which was the most recurring dream I had, and exactly what I did once I bounced off the shrubbery. Dad's beaming was always short-lived in my childhood.

But, master flying I did, much like the proverbial bird getting kicked out of its nest. That maiden flight lives on like a first ride on a bicycle without training wheels must be for other kids. I could see the pride dancing in my father's eyes as I stretched my arms out, tightening them as I sliced through the sky.

Unfortunately, that pride was short-lived. Soon after I began charging the kids at school a buck a flight.

June 19

Bullittproof told me today that I'm practically a thing of the past, that anyone one hundred percent anything is an endangered species.

He's referring to, of course, the fact that I'm a natural-born flyer, not an "accident" as he so thoroughly enjoys calling himself, or a half-human half-whatever.

I never thought of myself in percentages. My mother and father do both hail from the same side of the sun, a place where there is no nuance in skin color, no difference in dialect, no varying cultures. But, if you ask me, those are the things that I like about earth.

June 21

Just passed my downstairs neighbor shooting hoops with his son in the park. The kid was wearing new Flying Avenger Nikes. They flicker every time you go for a lay-up.

When I was a boy, father/son outings were difficult. My father always adhered to the rules of the game, while I had a tough time adapting my behavior to human-levels of acceptability. Pretending like one of my legs being in a potato sack impeded my performance, or acting like I couldn't simply blow the egg across the finish line with a blast of super breath. Dad would laughingly tumble onto the grass, feigning clumsiness so some puffing and wheezing parent could look like a star in his *F* student son's eyes as they crossed the finish line. For me it just wasn't that easy.

On one outing, in particular, he was none too thrilled when I hit a badminton birdie so hard the resulting whistle made several of our competitors' ears bleed into the homemade coleslaw. If you got it, flaunt it, was my philosophy.

Those get-togethers were awkward in other ways, as well, because many of the guys from my school spent large portions of the academic year lying about their fathers, and those lies would bite them on the ass on these days.

For instance, my friend Wayne said that his father was a Navy S.E.A.L. who spent his down time flying planes. It was obvious this wasn't true when Wayne Sr. pulled up in a van that read "Wayne Painting" on the side. The guy rolled out of the vehicle looking as if the closest he'd ever gotten to a Navy S.E.A.L. was that he may have eaten a seal at one time in his life.

I never understood that, either. Wayne Sr. seemed like a great guy, laughing and playing and looking after his son. My father did construction by day and single-handedly rid the streets of crime by night and neither really impressed me. It was the fact that he was always there that did. Even the morning after he stopped The Cavalier Cloner from destroying the world with an evil duplicate of the President.

June 24

Happy birthday to me.

My twelfth birthday was actually my favorite. I got my first costume. I had lobbied hard for one prior to that, particularly with a flashy cape, but my mom thought I was too immature. She cited my flying to the MTV awards without permission as an example. Of course, the picture I had taken with Debbie Gibson at the time made the extra few years of waiting worth it.

My first costume was okay, but there was no cape. This was the first time my father made his good guy/bad guy/cape comment, which really made an impact. An uncle of mine, however, pointed out how capes were a fictional faus pax, sartorial stupidity, and just plain trouble.

When I became of legal superhero age to make that decision for myself I immediately added a cape to my updated outfit, and quickly learned that my uncle was, in fact, correct. One wrong move and it's over your head like you're a hockey player in the middle of the fight of your life. I smacked the Statue of Liberty so hard I turned her torch upside down. It took my entire family to bend it back into place.

The color scheme of that first costume was better than I expected it to be, though. It was a dark blue with stripes of red criss-crossing everywhere. My mom was a top superhero costume designer, and her mom the inventor of the utility belt.

June 30

Today I saw the girl I rescued at the jewelry store a few weeks ago, but I was my alter ego at the time so she didn't look twice at me. It never ceases to amaze me how a simple pair of glasses can throw a person.

She looked lovely walking down the street, her hair up just so and her blue eyes shimmering in their sockets. We exchanged pleasantries and I couldn't help laughing about her obliviousness to the fact that we exchanged much more than that only a few weeks ago. Yes, I am the costume-clad hero who pried you from the clutches of danger. I am the one you deemed worthy of unrecipro-cated affection, of hero worship and idolatry. But, right now, on this sidewalk, during broad daylight, I am just another suit-and-tie guy seemingly vying for your attention. Too bad, 'cause I could have really used a blowjob.

I'm beginning to think that I'll never be completely happy.

My break-up with Diana still stings, even more so than the wound Doc Laser inflicted on me with his nose beam when last we tangled. Isn't that just hilarious? Still reeling from an ex's unmet demands and the break-up that resulted, while an actual battle atop the city's highest buildings as hundreds of innocent bystanders looked up in awe hasn't accrued any interest in my memory banks.

It's a bitter pill for a superhero: Overpowering everyone and everything but an ultimatum.

Seeing this stunning woman in her short business skirt, whom I saved and who swallowed, has made me reflect on all of the people in my life whom I didn't and couldn't connect with on a larger scale. To her I was nothing more than a snubbable peon, certainly not the swooping avenger of not even a month ago. What tunnel vision. Speaking of vision, it's moments like these that make me wish I had X-Ray.

Fourth of July

Just got in from an all-day party. July fourth is a tough day for superheroes. Some fireworks sound so much like fire*arms* that you just can't relax. And when a girl screams on top of that you're constantly on the verge of springing into action, which isn't as easy during the summer months, since it's impossible to wear a costume beneath a bathing suit.

A funny conversation took place around the picnic table involving me. Or, the other me, that is: The Flying Avenger (sometimes I'm not sure which me is the real me). Everyone was talking about how I stopped Sinisterio from taking over the entire city last winter. A couple of the guys played it down and made macho remarks that I ignored, at least until the volleyball match. Now I know why they call it a "spike." If hit hard enough, a volleyball can actually pierce a man's face and stick out like a dart.

The kids were the best part of the discussion. Their eyes were as wide as the volleyballs themselves as they talked about the near-legendary battle. Later, after everyone had exhausted the topic, a few of the kids wrapped beach blankets around their shoulders and pretended to fly across the back yard.

I couldn't help thinking it was crazy, though, that on a day that celebrates soldiers fighting for the very freedom everyone was enjoying, while they passed Frisbees beneath American flags, they'd be talking about me freezing Sinisterio with my breath.

July 10

Watched the Sci Fi channel for six hours straight today. How is The Incredible Hulk considered a superhero? He's a wanderer who transforms into an ignorant, lumbering, green monster and wreaks havoc until he can find a comfortable pair of pants again. How starving is the populace for heroes that they would consider this cretin one?

I changed the channel during a promo for *Sliders* and came across a news story about a mother who flipped her car over on a highway off-ramp. Her infant child was strapped into a baby seat in the back. Reportedly, the squeals of her terrified child provided her with an adrenaline rush that enabled her to lift the vehicle and pull the baby out.

I switched *The Hulk* back on. Someone had evidently angered his "human" form again, so The Hulk was standing before that person, vigorously flexing his muscles and making his breasts twitch, for whatever reason.

It's superhero week on the Sci Fi channel until Sunday night.

July 14

My boss is divorcing his fifth wife. At this point in time his arch-enemies outnumber mine.

The two major loves of my life were a complete contradiction of one another. My first, a childhood sweetheart of sorts, was far too demanding of my time for me to effectively use my abilities. She became suspicious of my disappearing acts, and essentially my superpowers began to be seen as a mistress.

So I entered into my relationship with Diana with every card on the table. I told her of my powers and she was ecstatic. She never wanted me out of costume. Have you ever showered while wearing boots? It's as uncomfortable as it is idiotic.

Eventually she left me when my climaxing stopped thrusting her across the room.

July 19

I read my blind date's mind tonight. Man, what a mistake. She went over recipes while I talked about my job, balanced her checkbook while I ordered the wine, and detailed what she'd do to the waiter as I was getting anecdotal.

I don't ordinarily do the mind-reading thing, either. I realize how invasive it is. Plus (which was yet again the case this evening), they're never thinking about what you hope and/or think they're thinking about.

A sales girl from the office set up the date and, in retrospect, her mind is the one I probably should have been reading. That way I could have heard the laughing as she went on about Princess Preoccupation's "zippy personality" and "ultra-important and demanding job" as a telemarketer. If super-villain is second to anything, it may be a telemarketer.

In college, I had a friend who constantly complained about women and often said that he wished he could read their minds so that he could finally figure them out. I always wanted to tell him that knowing what they're thinking only makes things trickier.

July 21

VH1's *I Love The 70's*. Whew! Marsha Brady, still hot. Lynda Carter, just not. I wonder if Wonder Woman is still pissed. She was never happy with Carter's casting.

Speaking of Wonder Woman, she is good-looking but I wouldn't date another superhero. It would be far too competitive.

"I saved the world today, what did you do?"

"Um, stopped a mugging."

I can appreciate having similar interests and being in the same line of work, but ultimately the high profile, media-fascinated nature of the gig would tear us apart.

I'll take a girl who bleeds any day.

July 22

One of those mornings where I wish I didn't have to go to work.

I honestly never grasped the concept of the superhero term "secret identity." Always smacked of oxymoron to me. This became increasingly frustrating with Diana, who only wanted The Flying Avenger around; she was besotted with him and completely uninterested in who I was out of costume. The most difficult of love triangles. (It is not lost on me that Diana continues to find her way into these entries.)

Nonetheless, my father used to sacrifice tried and true bedtime stories in an effort to communicate the importance of the secret identity to me.

One of his standby sermons involved a distant relation of mine, some showboat who subcontracted his powers every time the circus came to town. Foregoing any form of costume, he not only performed in the shows (matinees, even!) but also found his way onto the local news for pretty much every live broadcast or interview.

The story goes that a terribly ill woman caught the evening news and sought my cousin out. Seems she had always dreamt of flying and was determined that he grant her deathbed wish, so to speak.

And so he whisks her up into the clouds right in front of her house, his faux heroism as much a mask as the one he never wore.

Well, somewhere above the trees the woman began to vomit. Mister Flex-and-Smile-for-the-Camera paid no attention and she choked on it and died in his arms.

My problem with this story of dad's has always been that even in costume, this could have happened. But, I guess the point is that it wouldn't have resulted in ten to twenty.

July 29

I just saw Diana! It's amazing how this kind of thing always seems to happen when you're at your most unprepared. I swear, that time The Zombinator unleashed a legion of the undead on the city took me less by surprise.

I had ordered some take-out from the new Mexican place down the street, was just going to pop in, grab it, and be on my way, when there she was, in all her beautiful glory, and quite a bit less than alone. Introductions prevailed and soon enough I found myself losing my second battle in recent months, this one to jealousy. I began lacing the conversation with innuendo, every other remark a coy reference to my superpowers or some heroic deed I had done while dating her. She was getting it all, too. Suddenly I was feeling superior somehow, and not just because of my super powers, but because some semblance of a history existed. As a result, this ability to have two conversations right in front of this guy, with him unaware of the second, was possible.

How could he compete? I thought. *I can fly, I can read minds, I save lives in my spare time!*

Mortal men have no idea how that feels, life and death twitching in the palm of your hand, writhing like a fish on a hook. I became so self-absorbed I barely heard his pager go off, beckoning him back to the ER.

August 3

I just saw on the news that Blowhole escaped from prison earlier today. Super villains get far more press than superheroes, which I've always found disconcerting.

One thing's for sure, this isn't going to be good. I barely got him in there three months ago and he's already out, no doubt hell-bent on revenge—it's #2 on the super villain code of conduct for a reason.

He blew a hole in the side of his cell. What kind of judge places a super villain with a name like Blowhole into your average, run-of-the-mill prison anyway? Help me out here.

The last time we crossed paths was a doozie. Blowhole had managed to blast the vault door of Banner Bank clean off its hinges. If not for his bumbling henchmen he'd surely have gotten off with the entire cache. Their shenanigans bought me enough time to get to the bank and sufficiently get the entire situation under wraps, though it wasn't an easy undertaking at all.

Blowhole's insistence on using henchmen is a curiosity in and of itself. He's a seven-foot, nitro-for-blood, explosives-strapped-to-his-back bad guy, for the love of God. Why would he need assistance?

That's one thing the Sunday funnies and the fifties matinees got right: Villains do use henchmen, for whatever reason. And they usually are bumbling. Perhaps it's because there can't be any real hiring process, and compensation only takes place if the job gets done. I can't imagine that there's a real training ground, either, other than being a petty criminal prior.

Henchmen do the bad guys' bidding for a pittance of what's usually raked in, if they survive the whole affair at all. They are truly middle management.

August 6

Came home to a classic "Superman" episode on Nick At Nite after an unsuccessful attempt to uncover Blowhole's lair (superhero speak for "hideout," which is still superhero speak, for, well, house).

The whole Clark Kent ducking into a telephone booth thing still cracks me up. Why would we change into our costumes in telephone booths? They're certainly not roomy enough for such a feat, especially the boot end of the changeover.

The costume is a large part of the public fascination with superheroes, it seems. Through the years fiction has gone to great lengths to keep the flash intact, endlessly revamping and updating. Nowadays one could argue that a good percentage of fictional heroes boast costumes that are more trendy, runway-worthy fare as opposed to big-letter-on-the-chest, yellow boots and cape stuff. Super villain costumes have made even larger strides.

It's funny to note, too, that today's science fiction scribes seem intent on making the stars of their stories blend in and appear more and more like the guy (or girl) next door, only "with a vendetta." Since when do long leather coats constitute a costume? I mean, *seriously*. The line between hero and villain is increasingly thin.

But yeah, the superhero is alive and well; he just doesn't really have what one would call a tried and true costume anymore, which is probably a good thing because telephone booths are a thing of the past anyway.

August 9

It just dawned on me that Diana's new doctor boyfriend is the perfect resolution to our problem. He presides over life and death, makes money doing it, and has no alter ego. He's a doctor all day, every day. She probably makes him wear his stethoscope to bed. His specialty is rebound.

Diana loathed my "day" job, urging me to be in a constant state of Flying Avenger. I couldn't possibly be The Flying Avenger all day. Alter egos equal money. The only way to make money in a costume all day is if you're a villain, which is maybe what Diana wanted. During an argument once I told her that there is no paying gig for a superhero, never mind any privacy, so it's off to a lair with the occasional thievery for food and jewels and what not. Her response? "Sounds good to me." I thought she was joking at the time, but in retrospect, I'm not so sure.

Think about it. Once you become a villain you have to stay that way, all day. You don't bolt into a dark alleyway to put on your costume … and then control the universe. When you do control the universe you want everyone to know that it's you who does.

August 15

I have lost a battle with ultimatum. I was trounced by jealousy. But, loneliness … loneliness just might be the end of me.

August 15 (yes, again!)

I was really high tonight. I don't think that I have ever, ever flown so high. It felt good to not have to worry about birds like they were bugs aiming for my teeth, to rise above even the clouds, to feel the sun get closer and closer. I wasn't a superhero. I wasn't a super villain. I was just me.

Sometimes when I'm flying it's hard to believe that the earth is actually spinning, that anything at all is even taking place down there. And while I'm still curious as to what may be just outside the earth's orbit, somehow earth is enough for me.

The first time that I ever just went for a fly—no agenda, no dollar in my pocket for lugging a classmate along, no place to be that would take too long otherwise—it was awesome simply to watch everything get smaller and smaller beneath me. Even then, though, much as I wondered about what was further out there, it felt too good being on the top of something to push it and be at a bottom again, or even worse, a middle.

Tonight the stars fell like snowflakes towards me, and there was a stillness like the world had never stormed, like wars had never happened. Flying was the gift it was meant to be, not just something I was born able to do, some Point *A* to Point *B* thing. I was reminded how getting somewhere can be more fun than the somewhere itself, and for the first time in my life I understand why flying is the number one human dream.

August 19

It's all over the news how Blowhole has reduced the city to a constant state of fear. Bullittproof took him on last night, but when one of Blowhole's 8-ball grenades totaled Bullitt's costume he took off for his girlfriend's (in one of the photos in the newspaper you can see nipple). No one has heard from Bullittproof since.

"Blowhole Rules," "City Bows To Blowhole," and "No Stopping Blowhole." These have been some of the headlines. I haven't had headlines as powerful and seemingly positive as this in my entire career. "Hugh Jackman as Blowhole?" was just the tease on *Entertainment Tonight*.

I am in my costume as I write this, sans cape, about to soar above these familiar brick trees and mountains. My cape stares at me from the closet, like a girlfriend I have forsaken, taking turns wondering who'll be better off.

Jakes

by SEAN BEAUDOIN

"Hello. Golf World. Can I help you?"

"Yeah. Five thousand. Miami."

"Jesus, Ted," said the voice on the other end. "Again?"

"What?"

"I dunno if I can write that."

"Sure you can. Grab a pencil," Ted said.

In the background, phones rang, odds were quoted, because no one wanted to face Thanksgiving without some money down, a reason to live through another helping of stuffing and jarred cranberry sauce.

"I'm gonna have to get Marty," the voice finally said. "You know the drill."

Aside from being married to Ted's sister, Marty owned a hair restoration clinic and the small golfing accessory store that sat below it. In a tiny room with carpet like the sixteenth green, he took the local action.

"Ted?"

"Hey, Marty. Five grand. Miami."

"Yeah, I heard that already."

"So, what's the problem?"

"I guess the *problem* is that you're already down, what? Twenty-seven grand?"

"Twenty-six nine." Ted reminded him, stepping off his treadmill and wiping his neck with an orange towel. The machine made an awful sound, the bearings almost shot.

"Oh yeah, right. Twenty-six nine. How long's it been since you paid on any of that?"

A month ago, Ted's last patient had left him, a tiny woman who'd spent three years on the couch at a hundred an hour trying to work up the courage to move out of her mother's house. She marched into the office, handed him a dollar, said, "Here's a tip," and walked out, cured.

"A month?" Ted guessed, holding the phone in the crook of his neck. He got down on the floor and started doing sit-ups.

"Right. A month, Ted. Thirty days and no payment? Not kosher."

It was easy to picture Marty with a porkpie and a hand-rolled Cuban, looking all *Scorsese*. In reality, he was tall and thin, sinking putts into a mug, a bad hair restoration job spreading across his dome like a half-mowed lawn.

"Listen Marty, you gonna write it or not?"

Ted hit twenty crunches, a pain in his abdomen, and then rolled over into a sun pose.

"Also? Ted? What are you doing with five on the Dolphins? You've been betting Miami for a *year*, and they haven't covered *once*. Not a single *time*." Ted said nothing, gliding into downward-facing-dog.

"Even if they win, which they won't, you'll still barely make a dent in your principal. Why not find something with odds you like?

Six to one, maybe eight to one?"

"Ten grand, Miami." Ted answered, choosing a pair of hand weights.

"Up to ten now? Fine. Roll of dimes for the asshole. Got your slip right here. But you lose this one, the whole thing, *all of it*, is due tomorrow. I don't care if you have to sell a kidney."

Ted's shoulders burned. He threw the weights onto the couch. One bounced off the vinyl cushion and smashed the door of the display case in which his wife's swimming trophies used to sit.

"Hey, Marty?"

"What?"

"Save me some white meat."

The turkey dinner would take place the next afternoon, the whole family in tow: aunts, cousins—Marty and his hair plugs.

"That's funny, Ted. Funny Ted, my brother-in-law. You should do stand-up."

"I've got stage-fright."

Marty slammed down the phone.

***

Ted got up early, went for a run, and then made some eggs. After doing the dish, he showered, letting the scalding water poach his face and shoulders. At noon, he clicked on the tube. Pre-game, cheerleaders, ex-players trying to be clever in their expensive suits. The room was nearly empty, carpet and exposed wire, a few packing boxes, the odd Styrofoam peanut. Ted sipped a medium vodka and waited for kickoff.

By halftime Miami was down sixteen.

Ted poured heavily.

By the fourth quarter, the Dolphins were running out the

string, down twenty-six, another hand-off up the middle. The phone rang. It stopped and then rang again.

Ted grabbed his duffel from the couch and walked out to the car. Then he went back for the birdcage.

"Mr. Jakes ready to take a ride?"

The bird squawked happily and tried to nip his finger. It was an ancient macaw he'd been given by a patient named Avery Brundle who'd bounced three consecutive checks and offered either the bird or his watch in lieu of a fee.

"All I need is another Timex, Brundle."

"Then how about the bird?"

Ted held up the cage. "Does it talk?"

"Dildo," said the macaw calmly, readjusting his grip.

"See? I told you he was worth it," Brundle said. "Do we have a deal?"

Ted gave the bird a peanut and set him on the couch. "Yeah, fine. Call it square."

"Thanks, Doc."

Brundle lingered in the doorway, the waiting room behind him empty. "Um, Doc? You never told me what's wrong with me."

Ted looked up from the bird. "You're scared of everything. How's that for a diagnosis?"

"Kinda crappy, Doc."

"Well, it's a bird's-worth, Brundle. Next time, bring a dog and we'll figure out a way to blame it all on your mother."

***

Ted left the TV on the curb and considered setting the house on fire. It was possible there was some kerosene left in the basement, half a can Gena's lawyer had neglected to inventory.

One of the neighborhood children snuck around the Accord and peered at Jakes, who fixed him with a black eye, unblinking.

"Hey kid, you want a TV?" Ted offered. "Free?"

The boy sized it with a glance. "It's not even cable-ready."

"Of course," Ted marveled, tossing the remote onto the lawn.

"Dildo," said Jakes.

"Mister?" asked the child, holding onto the driver's side door.

"Yeah?"

"What's a ..."

"It's a fake penis, kid. Go home and have a sandwich."

Ted floored the Honda, aiming its nose toward the highway. It would take two days to get to Miami, which was plenty of time for him to figure out how the Dolphins were going to repay his thirty grand.

***

After handling the morning action, five minutes to kick-off and the lines still jammed, Marty closed shop. He gave out the last of the gift turkeys to his phone guys, Dean and Willie, thirty-pounders frozen so hard they might thaw by Christmas.

"Hey, thanks, Mistah Nicosio." Dean said.

"Yeah, for real, Mr. N." Willie echoed.

Marty waved cheerily, pulling away in his Lexus. When he was out of sight, Dean slid his bird down the wet macadam like a luge, where it picked up speed and slammed into a parked Toyota. Willie followed suit with a bowling motion, his turkey roaring down the hill in solo formation, doing untold damage to a new Ford.

Marty drove slowly, fiddling with the radio from one end of the dial to the other, every station either Johnny Mathis or some nose-ring wearing pseudo-punk threatening suicide. No middle ground was essentially what the world had come to, he decided. There was some safety in profit, but not much.

A rabbit shot across the road and Marty swerved, managing to catch it mid-bound. It lay motionless in the rear-view. The Lexus was the scourge of the rodent population of State Route 9: a flash of chrome, a flick of the wheel, mortality. It was a compulsion. Some people gambled. *That* was a disgusting habit. Marty treaded squirrels. What was the difference? He'd never placed a bet in his life. He worked hard and figured he deserved to let off some steam.

When she first found out, four months after their wedding, halfway to dinner and two raccoons already radialed, Marie had insisted on therapy.

"It's not normal, Mart. God's creatures deserve better."

"Normal is as normal does." He responded, eyeing a marmot lurking at the next intersection.

"I'm calling my brother." Marie announced.

"No chance," Marty said, accelerating.

"You're going," she told him. "Period."

Marie lit a cigarette.

"And slow down."

Marty lifted off the gas, gearing into low.

***

For six months, at two hundred an hour, Marty rode the couch, trying to put words to impulse to explain the clear, lucid joy of snuffing rodentia. Ted had been helpful, at first. Marty went on a regimen of behavioral control. He chewed Paxil like cashews.

"You know, I got to say, Ted, I think this is helping."

Ted refolded his form and circled a horse named *Penury's Loss*, who was running in the fourth. "Tell me more."

"I mean, when Marie asked me would I please do this, I wasn't so sure, you know?"

There was nothing in the fifth, a bunch of nags claiming for under a grand. Might as well close your eyes and throw a dart. "Any dreams lately?"

"Just bits and pieces. Like, I'm in a car and the brakes don't work? That kind of thing. Also, the one with my father again. Remember I told you? He's got a tail?"

"Right, right." Ted agreed. "Listen, Marty, times up."

"Already?"

"Yeah. Also, while you're here, I got a few slips for you."

By the second month, Ted's losses began to eclipse his fee. Then double. Then triple. Marty found himself in collection mode, instead of closing his eyes and working on hostility redirect. When Ted's sheet had swollen to ten grand, Miami having lost a half-dozen consecutive games, Marty pulled the plug.

"I may not be cured, but you're fucked," he said, slamming Ted's door for the last time. The population of Jersey voles took a marked downturn.

***

Ted's wife Gena couldn't help but notice the ebbs in their bank account. She taught tennis, the pro at the local club, undefeated, enormously powerful legs and shoulders capable of hammering the fuzzy yellow ball in unreturnable blurs. She'd come to Ted as a patient, who convinced her both of her beauty and the poor judgment of speaking in her natural baritone. In half a year, having risen a full octave, she left the couch as his wife.

"Marie says you're still writing slips through Marty?" Gena said, swinging an expensive graphite in the living room, back and forth in front of her Nikes. Tiny puffs of carpet fiber hovered. Ted set down his briefcase, tired after a long day of bald depressives and manic fondlers.

"I can always count on my sister to back me up."

"Marie's not your problem, Ted? Gambling is for the weak? All your clients know you're a deadbeat? Who trusts a compulsive psychiatrist?"

Gena instinctively phrased everything as a question, an affectation learned from years of defining oneself through the hierarchy of score. Did I win? Did I lose? By how much?

"Babe," Ted began, "it's under control, I swear."

"Horse-shit, Ted? I can't do this anymore?"

"Listen, I'll stop. I'll see someone. A *professional*."

"You'll never stop, Ted? Meanwhile, my serve has gone to shit? Before I know it you'll be hocking my rackets?"

Gena began to fill a suitcase with matching skirts and sweaters.

"I'll lay you ten to one this is a bluff." Ted told her.

"Physician, heal thyself?" She said, before slamming the door.

***

Marty idled while the Lexus whirred and pinged. It was possible some pelt had worked its way into the engine. His house was a green-sided duplex, set on a small rise, the manicured lawn and perfect shrubbery an exclamation of sobriety. Nothing out of place. Marty was ten years sober. He and Marie had found one another at a meeting, the two of them an industry of stickers and slogans, the air of having spackled certain flaws.

"Babe, what in hell are you doing?"

Marie was in the yard, raking leaves.

"It's called exercise, Mart. You should try it."

Marty got out and kissed his wife. He pulled up his tracksuit, which revealed a hairy paunch. "I look like I need to do sit-ups?"

"Yes."

A cold wind picked up trios of leaves and scattered them across the few sections she'd cleared.

"It's my mother," Marie admitted, "in there. Cooking."

"Kicked out of your own kitchen?" Marty sympathized

"It's *my* aunt. And *your* aunt. And all the cousins. Turns out everyone knows a better way to baste. *This is how they basted in the old country*."

"The old country?" Marty laughed. "What, Trenton?"

"Exactly." Marie said, dropping the rake. The tines vibrated oddly, a little song of defeat. "By the way, aren't you home early? Do I need to check the treads?"

Marty waved her off. "I gotta make a quick stop. Business."

Marie looked at him knowingly. "Not Ted? Don't tell me Ted. Not today."

"Ted." Marty admitted.

"I don't want to know." Marie told him, holding up her hands in defeat. "How much, or how deep, or whatever."

"Down another ten." Marty said.

"I told him last time. And the time before that."

"Yes, you did. And I told him no more free passes."

"Marty, he's my brother. It's Thanksgiving."

"Exactly."

They stared at one another, nothing left to confirm.

***

Marty picked up Danny Hands, his usual guy, at the Howard

Johnson's downtown. Hands was small and unimposing, skinny neck and polo shirt, you'd place him as a dentist, or maybe a waiter, if you noticed him at all. That made him valuable. That and his enormous mitts. Once he got hold of someone, no matter who, they never got loose. Body builder? Kung Fu moron? Going nowhere. Hands was worth twice what Marty paid him, and he knew it.

"Hey, boss."

"Heavy D." Marty grinned.

Hands said nothing, as Marty wheeled into traffic, gunning through an underpass filled with homeless, half the city sleeping in boxes and shopping carts.

"Ted's?" Danny guessed. Normally he wouldn't ask, but this was a situation that could get confusing. Who to grip and when. Family business was bad business.

"Ted's." Marty nodded.

A cat crouched by the side of the road. The car drifted across the yellow line, before righting itself.

Hands began to warm up. Thumb to pinkie, thumb to index, this little piggy, that little piggy. Marty was used to the routine now, but the first time he'd seen it, he thought Hands was off his nut. They were on their way to collect from a pair of Russians, twins who'd betted heavily on Tyson the night he went bat-shit and tried to eat Holyfield's face. The Russians figured they didn't owe due to an "act of god." Marty tried to explain that a disqualification was as good as a knock-out. They weren't buying it. They beat up his first collector, who to this day still shit into a tube, and then threatened to call some Chechen pals of theirs. Hands strolled into the house, fully warmed up, gripped them both at the same time, one deltoid each, and squeezed until they paid off. By midnight they were glad to. They even placed another bet. Rematch. Let it ride on Iron Mike. Also, every Christmas they sent Marie a bottle of excellent vodka, along with a card asking that Marty kindly relay their best wishes to the "big-fist man." You had to admire the Russians. Pragmatic. They knew when they were beat.

Several children stood in front of Ted's house as they pulled up.

What?" Marty asked them, looming in a trench coat and track-suit. The children shrugged, reluctant to move, a juvenile intuition for spectacle.

"Boo!" said Hands, expanding like twin parasols.

The children screamed and ran, a red-headed boy yelling "Dildo!" as they reached the woods in a pack.

Inside, Marty kicked at the few things left on the floor: a light-bulb, an orphaned shoe.

"Empty," Danny said.

"Stripped," Marty answered. "His wife took everything but the door-handles."

"Marriage," Danny said. "Not for me."

Marty had often wondered what kind of woman would be for him. Those fingers had to possess talents other than coercion. As far as he knew, though, Hands never did anything but watch movies on hotel cable.

"This was strictly punishment," Marty told him. "Caught him solid. He refused to even get a lawyer."

"*Kramer vs. Kramer*." Danny said, shaking his head, and then began to rummage in the refrigerator. "*War of the Roses*."

Marty had some contacts, guys that only bet NASCAR and ran strings of escorts out by the airport. He'd offered to arrange a few dates for Hands at cost, and was flatly refused. As Marty looked at Danny's back, he wondered for the first time if Hands was queer, envisioning sad-eyed men in dank bathrooms lining up to be gripped. It was too awful to contemplate.

"Yup, he's gone." Marty said, as he peered into rooms, each one more depressing than the last. He had a flash of sympathy for his brother-in-law, and then dismissed it like a streaking raccoon.

"*Marathon Man*," Hands said idly.

"C'mon, D, we're going."

Danny looked up, silhouetted in the blue light of the fridge. "Nothing in here. Soymilk. Tofu."

"Have a yogurt." Marty told him. "For the road."

***

Ted aimed the Honda toward the Keys. Thirteen hours later he was two hundred miles from Miami. He'd driven straight through, stone drunk, sipping half a case of light beer and feeding Jakes truck-stop Cheetos, only stopping to urinate and knock off a few hundred crunches at various roadsides.

He woke in the parking lot of the Dolphins' practice facility, no idea how he'd gotten there, shaky and tired, the sun already up and fogging the windshield. The Honda was neatly parked between dozens of enormous chrome SUV's, blinding light reflected off every surface.

Ted stood and stretched. "We're here," he told Jakes, who searched under his wing for nits, unimpressed.

Ted went to the trunk, selected a bone-handled hunting knife and slipped it into his jacket lining. He washed his mouth out with beer, using his middle finger as a brush, and then wandered unsteadily to the tall wire fence that surrounded three fields, coaches already coaching, some players unlimbering, a thin black girl marking off yard lines with a chalk roller.

The fence ran along the side of the building, an asphalt strip from the locker room to the first goalpost. There were a number of people already lined along it, low-cut blondes, a few kids waiting for autographs, some old women in sun hats and team jerseys they wore like dresses, dying to tell a player, any player, that they hadn't missed a practice since the Depression. Ted was the only male adult.

A door opened and the crowd pressed against the fence, calling the names of certain players. The men, all the size and shape of industrial boilers, wearily strolled the gauntlet, ignoring the fans. They limped and ached, already sweating, carrying helmets and shoulder pads and avoiding eye contact. A few raised heavily taped arms in a sort of general acknowledgement, and then trudged out of earshot. Ted watched the last of them go, trying to come up with a plan, as a large shadow enveloped him.

"Nice bird."

On the other side of the fence, within easy stabbing distance, stood a player, hair pulled in tight rows against his scalp. Tattoos peeked from under pads along his arms. He gave Ted a huge smile, gold fronts, one incisor set with a tiny diamond.

"Thanks."

"I dig birds. Though most times in a bucket, extra crispy."

Ted reached into his jacket and gripped the knife.

"Dildo," said Jakes.

The player laughed. "Tweety got some street in him, huh?"

Ted laughed, too, unable to help himself.

"So what 'chu want, huh?" The player asked. "An autograph?"

"I wanna know if you played last weekend." Ted asked, fingering the blade. "Thirty-six to three? You in on that one?"

The player sighed. His voice became softer. "My name's Bevins," he said, showing Ted the lettering across his mammoth shoulders. "I'm third-string? I haven't played in two years. You think if I was any kind of name, I'd be standing here talking to you?"

"You dropped the Ebonics."

Bevins grinned. "I know. I was just screwing with you. It usually scares the white boys away."

"It almost worked," Ted admitted.

"Listen, I gotta go practice ... not that they're missing me, but I want to ask you a question. You're the first normal to talk to me in, like, *forever*."

"Normal?" Ted laughed, dropping the sweaty knife and letting it fall back into the lining of his jacket. "Shoot."

"Why are these people here?" Bevins asked, not a trace of irony in his voice. This was the first time in years someone asking Ted a question, really wanting an answer.

"I mean," he continued, "I'm just some drop-out from USC, right? All season, every practice, they stand here and scream. Why? They don't have a wife and kids? They don't have friends?"

"That's a tough one, Bevins."

"Three years at Southern Cal," Bevins grinned, "and people think all I learned is how to hit people."

"Listen," Ted said, feeling that this was suddenly important, "I know you're still fucking with me."

Bevins grinned. "Maybe a little."

"But I'm gonna answer you, anyhow. See, I came here to pay off a debt. A heavy debt. Now I think I'm going to impart some wisdom instead. You too street to hear it?"

"Lay it on me." Bevins answered, no longer smiling.

"Everyone needs something to believe in, right? Okay, that's obvious. But I think we've just gotten to the point that believing doesn't work anymore. Too many moving parts, you know? The Holy Trinity or the president or whatever. Too many angles. Contradictions. But big guys in blue outfits? Now you're talking. A game. Someone wins and loses. No surprises. In the end, it hurts too much to want more."

"That's some deep shit, bird-man," Bevins said, nodding. "But, yeah, I can see it."

"I mean, me, personally? I don't know what to believe," Ted rubbed his eyes with the heels of his palms. "My wife left me. Eight years and then she split. Now it's just me and the bird."

Bevins poked his finger through the fence. "Well, if it helps, I'll tell you something now, huh?"

Ted nodded.

"One, you're okay, white bread. And I mean that. Two, Ed Bevins believes in his momma and his bank statement. Period."

"What about all this?" Ted asked, extended his hand to take in the fields and players, the cheerleaders and coaches and the highway, far in the humid distance, a road out of Miami and everything beyond.

Bevins squinted, spit a stream of tobacco, and then began to trot away, his cleats making an odd sound on the softening tar.

***

Two weeks later, Ted sat in a lawn chair in front of his favorite cabana bar. He'd been there the day before, and intended to be there the day after. His skin had turned a lustrous brown. He did yoga for two hours every morning at the edge of the water, and then claimed his recliner, a convenient six feet from the closest wait station. He'd become friendly with a few locals, explaining that he was a retired magician from Vegas who sold all his props and gave up the life. "How many starlets can a guy cut in half?" He'd ask wearily. If nothing else it explained Jakes.

When a man sat just behind him, Ted assumed it was Bertram, a Jamaican who sometimes cadged a few beers and liked to talk philosophy. The Neitzschean waves. The Hegelian sun.

"Nice bird."

Ted craned his neck, surprised. No patois. No dreadlocks. It was a short, absurdly pale man in a tennis outfit.

"Thanks."

Jakes slept peacefully, his cage half-covered with a towel. The man looked like he'd spent his entire life preparing to extract a molar. He had the largest hands Ted had ever seen.

"Ted Warner, retired magician."

"Danny," Hands responded. He removed his shoes and ran his toes in the sand. "For a guy that hits the sauce this early, Ted, you're in pretty good shape. You know it?"

Ted looked down at his wiry frame. "Push-ups. My personal secret."

"Cutting edge," Danny said. "Really."

Ted grinned and signaled for two drinks. "Listen, you might want some of this, too." He held up a bottle of lotion. "You're already red. Twenty minutes, it's lobster. Half an hour: third degree."

Hands squirted some and managed to cover almost his entire body in one pass. "Listen, you think you could do my back?"

"Dildo," Jakes said, waking up.

A cell phone rang, and Danny pulled it off his belt, not bothering to answer. "It's for you." He said, handing it to Ted, who put it to his ear.

"There he is, the comedian," Marty growled, sounding like he was ten feet away.

Ted sighed.

"How's the beach?" Marty asked.

"Clean," Ted answered "Not dirty. Not Jersey."

Jakes squawked loudly.

"Ted, you know that birds are filthy animals, right?"

"I figured you liked birds," Ted hissed into the mouthpiece. "Bald eagles, maybe. Whole new market for hair plugs."

Danny laughed.

"Ted, what are you doing, huh?" Marty asked, all business. "Where you think you're going?"

"I'm not going. I'm here."

It felt good to say that. He chewed ice from his empty glass.

Marty sighed. "It's like you're *asking* for a tune up, you know it?"

"A tune up," Ted laughed. "Who says that? Tune up? That's a movie no one saw."

"*Untouchables*," Hands said, "DeNiro."

"Okay, but Miami, Ted? Miami?" Marty asked.

"Listen, I'll pay you back," Ted promised. "Installment plan. I'm gonna put out the couch soon. Maybe you can come back in and we'll talk squirrel."

"I told you, remember? You had to make good, and what did you do? You ran."

"I figured something out, Marty. I mean it. It's like a godsend that all this happened, you know? I finally got my head right."

Hands reached out and touched Ted's knee. "You're funny, you know it?"

"Listen, are you trying to be funny?" Marty practically screamed.

"No, I'm serious," Ted explained. "I talked to a Dolphin."

"Put Hands on the line," Marty growled.

Ted gave the phone to Danny, who listened, nodded, and then gave it back.

"Hey, I'm sorry," Danny said. "Really," and then reached into the cage and gripped the bird. Mr. Jakes lay at an odd angle.

"That wasn't necessary," Ted whispered into the receiver.

"Okay, then what is, huh?" Marty said. "You tell me what's necessary, Mr. Thirty-six thousand nine hundred."

Ted looked out at the ocean. It was a lifetime to the first breaker.

The waiter, a tiny Cuban in a bow-tie, came over with the drinks. He put them next to Jakes. "This supposed to be a tip?"

Hands gave him a twenty.

"Health inspector," the waiter said, not moving. "Dead fowls."

Hands gave him another twenty, and he went away.

"Turkey dinner was good, Ted," Marty said. "No one asked about you. No empty place settings. You're practically a ghost, you know it?"

Hands reached over and squeezed Ted's wrist. The pain was excruciating.

Ted picked up Mr. Jakes with his free hand, caressing the marbled feathers. "Am I going home, Marty? Is that where I'm going?" The bones in his wrist were fused, white hot.

"Yeah, Ted, Hands is taking you home. I'm sure there's plenty of leftovers. Hands will make you a white-meat sandwich."

"Cranberry sauce and everything?"

"Cranberry sauce and everything."

Ted moaned, dropping Jakes in the sand while being led toward the car. He had a sense of deja vu, of being twelve and pulled around the state fair by his father, up and down the midway, bells and whistles, vaguely afraid of the pirate ride.

Namith's Mission

by JON MICHAEL McCARRON

Jacob's wake-up call came in the form of three sharp raps on the hollow motel door.

Instantly awake, he lay very still trying to glean what he could from the shadow spilling under the door and the noises outside his room.

One person. A man most likely.

The shadow moved.

A *big* man. This was not good.

Silently, Jacob cursed the god he had years ago declared dead.

He couldn't hear anything from the hall.

BAM. BAM. BAM. The door shook again. Jacob watched as hunks of paint flecked off onto the worn carpet.

"Quien es?" Jacob called out, moving silently toward the door. He walked in socks as close to the wall as possible to avoid the creaking floorboards.

"Con permiso! Deseo hablar a Jacob Nitti."

No. This was not good at all.

No one was supposed to know he was here, yet obviously he'd

made a mistake somewhere. Somehow in the whole process of ripping off his capo to the tune of fifty large and then stealing the poor bastard's wife (just to add insult, ya see?) he'd misstepped. Maybe it was the gas station attendant in Jersey that looked at him funny. Latrice told him it was only because he hadn't tipped. But what about the pharmacist in Atlanta? When he picked up Latrice's prescription he'd definitely gotten a nod. It was small but the man had nodded. And didn't he have just the hint of a smile? That fucker was smiling, alright. Smiling and laughing as he'd picked up the phone and started dialing while Jacob walked to the car. Jacob had wanted to go back and introduce them both to Mr. Black. Take them for a little walk, as we used to say, Jacob thought. But Latrice had insisted and shit, this whole thing was for her when you really looked at it, wasn't it? That being the case and Latrice ruling his heart, at least two of Borgata's leeches got to keep breathing.

"Jacob Nitti?" the voice came again.

"Quien es?" Jacob called again as he approached the kitchenette table. Reaching under, he peeled off the electrical tape that he had put there two weeks ago and produced his .45. The heft of black steel calmed Jacob a little. No matter what was about to happen he'd go down fighting.

"Sé hablar solamente con Jacob Nitti."

Damn. There didn't seem to be any way around this. Oh well, old boy, Jacob thought. Nothin' to it but to do it.

Jacob made his way to the door and crouched, placing the barrel of the gun against it about waist high. Somebody was aching to get gut shot and Jacob was more than willing to oblige.

"Who are you?" Jacob asked.

"Mister Nitti? I'm a friend. Latrice sent me."

"Gosh, pal. I'm afraid you got the wrong guy. I don't know any Latrice."

"She's told me your situation. I can help if you let me."

Jacob gently pulled the hammer back on his little friend.

"Buddy, I'm afraid I'm not the trustingest man in the world right now. Unless you got more than talk you're gonna have to leave or we're gonna take a little walk together you and I. And trust me when I say that you don't want that," Jacob's left index finger slid off the housing and wrapped gently around the trigger. "But right about now I do. In fact it's hard to think of something in this shitty world that I want more."

"What about a postcard from Latrice?" the man countered.

Jacob held his breath. This guy knew about the postcards. How much else did he know? The postcards, after all, had been the plan. Each town Jacob moved on to he'd send a blank postcard to Latrice's backroom alley apartment that was a secret to even Borgata himself. Jacob had worked this system out. At least that's what he told himself. He'd actually subconsciously cribbed the idea from a shoplifted *True Crime Stories* magazine years ago. After two weeks he'd move on to the next shithole motel in the next backwater town and he'd start the dance over again. It was his way of letting the heat die down. As long as the Wells Fargo wagon kept rolling and those couriers were not stayed from the swift completion of their appointed rounds, he could sleep at night.

Standing, Jacob unlocked the deadbolt and slowly opened the door while keeping the gun pressed against it.

The man in the hall was at least a head taller than Jacob's five feet and seven inches. Graying hair was swept back into a ponytail and the man's bright eyes were beset with a pair of silver pince-nez glasses. The man smiled politely down at Jacob. Around his neck he wore the collar of the righteous.

"Jacob? I'm Father Namith. May I come in?"

"Not just yet, friend. You say you have a postcard. I want to see it. And be real easy about it, eh?"

"Of course," the man nodded, reaching into his black suit coat. Jacob watched the man's eyes. Jacob had learned long ago that if there's going to be trouble you'll see it in a man's eyes before he even knows it himself. A man's reptilian brain will have made the fight or flight decision while his higher brains are still trying to forge a rational and nonviolent solution.

Father Namith produced a small piece of paperboard. One side featured someone's idea of a comical take on Munch's *The Scream*. The figure still had its hands clapped to its ears but it now had a dialogue bubble, like in a comic strip, that read, "Is it Friday yet?!?" Jacob didn't laugh. Instead he reached out between the door and the jamb and snatched the postcard from the priest's hand. Flipping it over, Jacob was greeted by a field of white and a postage stamp. When the Post Office had processed the card someone had rubber-stamped a cartoon snowman that now waved gleefully at Jacob Nitti. "Greetings from far, far away!" it read. It was addressed to a P. O. Box in Nova Scotia.

"Come in, Father," Jacob said, as he closed the door and undid the chain.

***

"Would you like somethin' to drink, Father?" Jacob asked. "The water's cold and tastes like copper and I have some beer but it's on the warm side I'm afraid." He cracked open the can he was holding and sat across from the priest at the kitchenette table.

"I'm fine, Mister Nitti. Thank you."

Jacob grunted. He dug into his pocket and pulled out a small brown bottle. After a minute of twisting and pushing he managed to get it open. Jacob peered into it with one eye, lips moving. He quickly dumped the contents into his palm and popped the lot into his mouth. He followed it with two glugs of warm beer.

"What was that?" The priest asked.

"Vitamins," Jacob replied.

"Are you sick?" The priest probed.

"Very."

"Is it a cold?"

"It's the human condition. Listen, do you know why Latrice sent you?" Jacob asked brusquely.

Father Namith ran a hand back through his hair. "I suppose I don't have a satisfactory answer for that. All I know is she said she needed my help and that I was the only person she trusted."

"No offense, father, but you're not exactly the kind of guy I expected."

The priest smiled and gave Jacob a small "What can you do?" shrug.

"Still," the priest said, "I'd like to help however I can."

Jacob sighed.

"Fine. Shit. Fine. It don't matter now anyway I suppose. Um." Jacob paused to collect his thoughts. "Why don't you tell me what Latrice told you? We'll start there and I'll see what I can fill in."

"Well, *Reader's Digest* version? You and Miss Latrice are *close* friends and you have stolen both her and a rather large sum of money from a fairly nasty man named Borgata. While I don't travel in your circles, even I know who he is, and so the two of you are, wisely, currently in hiding while his associates look for you. Oh, and you're an enforcer. She didn't tell me that part, but I've pieced it together."

Jacob's eyes narrowed slightly. "What do you know about enforcers?"

Namith held up a hand offering peace.

"Sorry. That's a rather archaic term I suppose. If I've given offense I apologize sincerely. Is there a term you prefer I use?"

Jacob stared for a moment, thinking.

"Forget it. Go on."

The priest shrugged. "You handle family business on the record. If someone isn't toeing the line, as it were, you remind them that even crime has rules. Is that about right?"

"It's about as polite as I've ever heard it," Jacob said. "Bottom line, Father, I hurt people. And God forgive me ... I like my job."

Jacob looked down. Atheist or not, he still felt an inbred sense of shame telling his sins to this man of the cloth.

"Did Latrice say anything else?"

"Yes. She said she loves you."

Jacob let this sink in for a moment. Something wasn't quite Jake.

"Forgive me, Father, but I'm a suspicious man by nature. Exactly when did she pass along all this information to you?"

The priest knitted his brow in thought.

"Well, I suppose it's been perhaps six or seven months. I'm afraid my memory isn't what it once was. She said that if a goodly time had passed and I hadn't heard from her I should use, oh, what were her words? 'All the powers of the Holy Church to find the man I love and do as he asks?'"

Six or seven months. It fit the timeline. The guy's story seemed legit, Jacob thought. Shit. It's really gonna happen.

Jacob nodded as an angry tear slid from his left eye. He brushed it away with the back of his hand.

"This is so tragic it's perfect, you know, Father?" Jacob laughed, which soon turned into more tears of anger.

The priest looked at the floor, not knowing what to say.

Jacob composed himself after a few moments and wiped his

eyes. Sucking snot to clear his nose, he spit the collected mucus on the stained linoleum with a hard thwapping sound.

"You smoke, Father?" Jacob asked.

The priest nodded and pulled a pack of Luckies from his hip pocket. Jacob chuckled.

"Luckies, Father? Tsk."

The priest handed Jacob a smoke and lit one, chuckling to himself.

"I know, I know. I never hear the end of it from my wife. I can't even smoke in my own house any more. That's a pretty sad situation, don't you think?" Namith's henpecked and weary smile was genuine.

"Terribly sad. Fuckin' pathetic." Jacob chuckled.

The two men enjoyed their cigarettes in silence for a few minutes, looking everywhere but at each other. The blue-white smoke danced between them, and turned the air acrid. When the priest had stubbed out his butt in the ashtray next to the sleeping pistol he looked at Jacob. Jacob felt the eyes but continued smoking anyway. He sighed to himself.

It was time.

Nothin' to it but to do it.

"Father, there was something Latrice didn't know. Why she had you come here, I mean. That was part of the plan. See? I had this whole thing worked out. I asked her to make this request on my behalf. I haven't spoken to God or been to Mass in forever so I hardly felt I had the right to make the request myself," Jacob trailed off.

"I have no right to make a request like this, do I?" Jacob quietly wondered to himself.

Namith thought a moment and then leaned conspiratorially toward Jacob.

"You have as much right as anyone. That's what God's here for.

Can I tell you a secret? Even the devil is a Christian."

Namith winked at this last piece of wisdom.

Jacob took this in and was heartened by the cryptic missive, at least enough to pick up his trail of thought and continue.

"I had her do this because I figured there'd come a point where I was sick of running. And now I am. I just want to be done with it. I'm tired, Father and I want you to help me."

"Of course I will," said Father Namith.

Jacob looked at the priest in the fading light that filtered through the yellowed window shade.

"I'll be dead in a few hours and I want you to tell me it's ok. You know. To go."

The priest looked at Jacob in shock. Searching for words, he ran the last few minutes through his head, suddenly locking onto Jacob's meaning.

"Vitamins?"

Jacob smiled humorlessly.

"Oh, Jacob," the priest began, "suicide isn't the answer to anything."

"Please. Just save it," Jacob said, standing and walking away. "I've come to terms with many things in my life and I now realize everybody's gonna be a lot better off with me out of the game. Gimme another smoke will ya? It's not like they'll give me cancer."

Jacob grinned again.

"Jacob, please..."

Jacob wheeled on the priest and grabbed the gun.

"Listen, padre, I really appreciate you taking the time to come out here and give me Latrice's card, but don't think this is a chance to sermonize me. I gave up on God a long time ago, but I'm a superstitious man and you will hear my confession and give me absolution or you will leave. There will be no discussion of me not dying.

It's gonna happen. You accept that here and now or, by holy hell, there will be a shitstorm in this room tonight, and I will rain your fucking gray matter all over my bed before I go. Do. We. Have. An. Under. Standing?" Jacob tipped the gun barrel on each syllable to emphasize his point. Namith was silent for a moment. Then he nodded in grim shock to Jacob.

Jacob smiled and tossed the gun back on the table.

"Thank God it's Friday," Jacob began to laugh.

***

"Sit down, Father. Make yourself comfortable," Jacob said, reclining on his bed.

Father Namith moved a chair from the kitchenette to the foot of the bed and sat. "Forgive me faddah for I have sinned!" Jacob intoned.

Namith simply stared.

Jacob laughed. "Oh come on! You gotta have a sense of humor about this shit. You can't be a God groupie 24/7!"

Namith looked on. "If you're going to kill yourself, fine. So far you haven't impressed upon me that it would be any true loss to the world. How's that for not being a groupie? You want human? You got it, pal. But just as you had a caveat, so have I. You will use this time to speak seriously or I will walk out that door. "

Jacob's lips pursed. He wanted this confession. Hell, he *needed* it, didn't he? So stop being an asshole and let the man do his job so you can do yours, he thought.

"Ok, Father. Fair enough."

Namith tipped his head and straightened his jacket.

Jacob fidgeted with his smoke for a moment before beginning.

"Father," Jacob began, but the gravity of the situation weighed in and he started over penitently, "Forgive me, Father, for I have sinned. I can't remember the last time I made confession." With a sigh, he pushed on. "I'm a drunk and a cheat and a murderous liar. I've killed many people, men and women both, to get ahead in my profession, and I remember every name. Every face. I see them when I close my eyes."

Jacob broke off, his throat suddenly tight for some odd reason. He cleared it after a moment and continued.

"I've blasphemed and I've given up on God. I fell in love with my capo's wife and I stole money from him. I'm not a very good human being. I remember my mom. Bits of her. She was a good human being. She was caring and decent and kind and everything I'm not. My very existence is a stain on her memory. My sister Annie won't even return my calls. Did you know that, Father? I love that kid with my very heart and she won't even acknowledge me. Which I deserve. Granted. But it hurts Father. Latrice. I mean I love Latrice. I'd die for Latrice. But Annie? I'd kill for Annie. Coming from a stone killer, I guess that don't sound as much as it means. But it's true."

Jacob trailed off.

Father Namith lit another cigarette. The two men sat in silence. After a minute Jacob began again.

"As you can imagine, my height was something of a roadblock in my career. Tough guys are just that. Tough. Tough and big. Size don't matter in the practical sense. I mean, I could kill you just as dead as any six foot two asshole, but, like any other profession, appearances are important. And the other boys knew this. They rode me unmercifully about it. 'Hey, boss. How come you gonna give Jacob this cherry assignment? You know he can't make the killshot. Best he can hope for is to blow out the fucker's knee!' 'Hey, boss. You send Jacob out collecting money, someone's liable to take him for the paperboy!' They'd howl with laughter at this stuff.

Buncha unfunny young turk guinea fucks. If you're gonna be mean, at least be funny. I don't think that's too much to ask. Do you, Father?"

"No. No I don't."

Jacob harrumphed and continued.

"Mainly it was this one guy in particular. Joey Barilla. He was relentless. It was worse than grammar school, dig? I put up with it for awhile, 'cause Joey was one of Barilla's cast of regulars, as it were.

"This guy was always giving me shit about my height. Thought he was a real comedian, this guy. Getting my balls busted, I can handle. But what I can't handle is someone else getting involved in my business. I won't get into the messy details, but let's just say that Barilla took some money out of my pocket and so I had to take him for a little walk.

"That got me called in. I figured I was a dead man. It was Borgata himself wanted to see me. No fuckin' around with lieutenants or nothin'. 'Jacob,' he says, 'You do good work for me here. I ask you to give someone a reminder, you do that. I ask you to collect a vig, you do that. I don't care what your damage is or what gods you pray to, but I cannot have you seeking off-the-record revenge killings. How small is your pride that a babbo like Joey Barilla can get you seeing blood?' And I didn't have an answer for him."

"He says, 'Tell you what I'll do. You come out of the game for a bit. Let cooler heads prevail. Joey Barilla did have friends, you know? You come sit with me for a bit and maybe they forget this. Hey, in fact, I got a job for you. A special job.'"

"And that's how you met Latrice," Father Namith concluded.

Jacob looked down and nodded. "That was a year ago."

"So if you hadn't killed Barilla ..."

"Exactly, Father. I told you didn't I? A classic tragedy."

"So then what happened?"

"I dunno. Nothing special, I suppose. The oldest story. I was her girlfriend. I took her shopping. Borgata hated theatre so I ended up being a proxy date a lot of the time. I just looked after her in general. After a few months, I didn't miss my work. Sure, I'd run into the guys at the house. They'd tell me, oh, 'You shoulda seen the job we had last night,' or 'Hey, some new player calls himself Eddie Knives is moving on the Baker Boys! He's dead and he don't know it yet!' or 'War council tonight! Sure you can't make it, Jacob?' They seemed to respect me more since Barilla was dead. I kinda got the feeling some of them were actually afraid of me. Like if they said the wrong thing I'd take *them* for a little walk," Jacob laughed. "But I don't think I woulda. Just being with Latrice took a lot of that anger away. You know? But as much as I love her, she made me soft. She made me human again. And for that I can never forgive her."

"I think I can see that. My wife has the same effect on me. I think it's just part of being male. I think," Father Namith smiled, "I'd even call it part of the human condition."

Jacob stared blankly for a moment before he began laughing.

"You're ok, Father. I like you."

"You know, Jacob, I'm a bit surprised to say it, but I think I like you, too."

Jacob smiled weakly.

"It wasn't too long after that she started talkin' 'bout us leavin'. That we'd never really be together as long as Borgata was breathin'. I may have been in love, but I wasn't stupid. I told her in no uncertain terms that I simply didn't have the juice to whack her old man. She sulked for a bit and I got no love for a while. Then, one night, after a few too many, I tell her I know how we can do it. We just needed to wait 'til Borgata asked me to collect another vig. Then the two of us could just leave and have plenty of startin'-over money. At least, that was the plan."

"So it was her idea," Namith said. "Jacob, I have to say you have had the worst streak of luck I've heard in some time."

"Tell me about it."

Silence filled the room.

Jacob looked up at the priest. "So? Do I get it? Do you forgive me?"

Namith sighed heavily. "Yes, I do, son. I do. And who knows? Maybe I talk to *my* capo and I put in a good word."

The priest winked.

Jacob nodded twice and his eyes got wet. "Thanks, Father."

The priest nodded back and waved his hands, muttering in Latin.

"Just one more thing. Will you stay with me? Until, ya know, I'm gone?"

"I don't generally approve of euthanasia. Catholic thing, you understand? But, I don't suppose it could hurt to help a man in pain feel comfortable."

"I said you were an ok guy, didn't I?" Jacob asked. The priest smiled.

Nothin' to it but to do it, Jacob thought.

Reaching under his pillow, he pulled out a plastic dry cleaning bag. He studied it for a minute. Finally at peace with his decision, Jacob pulled it over his head and secured it with a rubber band around his neck.

"It shouldn't be long, Father. I'm already tired. I don't want to burden you any more than I have to."

"No burden, son. Trust me. In my long life, I've dealt with more pain than I care to think about. Just rest now. I'll sit and watch."

"Father, do you think Latrice knows I love her?"

Jacob's voice sounded alien through the plastic.

"Have you told her you do?"

"I've tried. But I don't think she hears me, really."

Namith smiled. "Even when it seems they aren't listening to us, they are, Jacob. Now rest, son," Father Namith cooed.

Jacob's breathing became rhythmic and the sound of the bag crinkling in and out with every breath became almost hypnotic, Namith thought. A cadence of life, or death really, as it were. He tilted his head.

It wasn't happening fast enough. Jacob felt like he was drowning. His eyes opened. Natmith pulled back in surprise.

"Little help here, Father?" Namith moved almost without realizing. He pushed the plastic down onto Jacob's face and pinched Jacob's nose closed. The body convulsed but Namith held him down with rapt attention.

Then there was no movement. The priest removed his hands.

Father Namith stood over Jacob Nitti's body for a moment, studying his face through the bag. With his right index and middle fingers he checked Jacob's carotid artery for a pulse. Ten seconds went by with no result. The old priest sighed slightly and walked to the phone. Picking up the receiver, he slowly punched eleven buttons. After a moment, the other end of the line was picked up.

"Yes. Borgata please."

Silence.

"Mister Borgata. Eddie Knives. Yes. Yes, I've taken care of the problem."

Eddie glanced at Jacob's body.

"Yes sir. No question. It'll look like a suicide. Thank you, sir. Very kind of you. No, I haven't found her as yet, but I will soon."

Eddie hung up the phone.

"Jacob, my boy," Eddie said, "You did the right thing. I respect you for that. And because of that, I'm just gonna let someone find you. I think you deserve that much, you traitorous piece of shit."

Eddie spit on the floor. "The best part is that now you're dead I can just tell Borgata you spent all his cash, which in turn makes me one rich cocksucker."

Eddie Knives walked to the kitchenette. All he had to do now was find the money. It would be close by. Weak men like Jacob always needed to know their prize was just within reach. It shouldn't take long to find, he thought.

Eddie sighed to himself as he began his search, "Thank God it's Friday."

Empire of One

by CARL MOORE

Kep Hatchy began to multiply when I was still in elementary school. There was little time to determine the facts, but the popular telling is that, while walking home from his job at the mega-mall, dressed in a leather trenchcoat that hid his fast-food uniform, Kep ate a bottle of pills he found in a ditch outside Culus Air Force Base. It multiplied him. There were two, then four, then eight of him, and he was instantly able to control all of what we have come to call "his-selves." They checked each other's acne patterns, random body hairs, chicken tendons between their teeth—anything that confirmed that they were all the same person. Sure enough, everyone was him. A nearby airman is reported to have heard all the Keps laughing together, saying, "Oh my God dudes, this is some rad, high-level action." They multiplied more—eight, sixteen, thirty-two. Within a few hours, there were hundreds, then thousands. They didn't have to run to take over the city, they just multiplied, took up space, and out-moped everyone who tried to stop them.

The government did not tolerate Kep's oppressive population. War followed, with hot chunks of metal spurting through gasses that burned everyone's eyes, even when we were hiding in our basements. I spent a year like that at the beginning of puberty while the adults fought with Kep, taking hisselves seriously enough to mobilize all of the armed forces, including the reserves. They tried to kill Kep quickly and in accordance with international law. The president launched an admirable effort to avoid genocide against Kep; to keep people from calling the POW camps "Kep-keepers" and the soldiers "dekepitators." But it dragged on and wearied them. Commanders despaired at Kep's strategies—how he blocked the road with hisselves until he was a shield of his own corpses for hisselves bringing up the rear; how he prevented tanks from seeing where they were going and clogged their treads with stringy tendons; how legions of Keps stood on runways, keeping F-14s from taking off.

Kep kept on and won the war by dying. He multiplied and died and buried hisselves, his blood flooding everything. In our food and on the bathroom floor, we found pieces of him. We screamed and called for the police to pick up the desiccating portion of Kep-multiple in our house. Kep's flat voice answered for the dispatcher, and he sent two of hisselves over to our apartment to help the three of hisselves who were already sitting around the stoop, ready to clean his parts out. The place stayed clean about fifteen minutes. We started calling it our fifteen minutes free of fame.

He always came back. If I closed my eyes, I heard him breathe. If I covered my ears, I smelled his waft of Naugahyde and grease. If I plugged my nose, I tasted his fingers putting something fried in my mouth. And if I closed that too, I started to suffocate. This last option would have been a good one, except that Kep's image swam in my oxygen-deprived daze, a montage of the ways I had seen him massacred, ways his cheap blue eyes had already met eternity a million times. My suicide attempt was doomed to end in frustrated gasps.

And that's when I got to see Kep. He puttered around nearby, aware of me, but not really caring what I did. He made hisselves less conspicuous when he wanted to, but the one thing he could never do was go away.

Business executives, politicians, famous entertainers, and generals all loathed Kep. He was not interested in money or in any of the bribes these people offered him in order to leave them alone. They didn't even appreciate the fact that he never fought back, and when his assumption of power was undeniable, he let them keep their positions of rank, not molesting them, interrupting them, saying or doing anything, other than hanging around their houses and riding in the back seats of their cars.

Kep provided crews of hisselves to repair the damage after the war. He let people go back to work and school and made sure people without jobs got enough to get by. Some complained that Kep was a Communist, though this couldn't be true—gradually, the malls reopened and people showed up to buy t-shirts and plastic lamps without Kep's interference.

An international group of delegates formed the Kep Council, headquartered in the United Nations building in New York. The United States was forced to admit its own weapons research had gone awry and turned one of its citizens into the first worldwide tyrant. A delegate from Japan is noted for commenting, "Why is it when America gives something to the world it always comes from a mega mall?"

Kep never said anything to the Kep Council, but he went to all of their meetings.

***

In spite of what everyone saw as the ongoing damage of Kep's reign, I considered my life to have an intuitive antidote to his presence. My job was an incidental circumstance, there to pay the bills so that I could spend more time at my girlfriend Tasha's Tai Chi class. On weekends, we'd read short stories aloud then head for the kitchen to attempt the perfect consistency of grilled asparagus. Our activities made for a somewhat hermetic existence. Barely twenty years old, we both dropped out of college when it dawned on us one morning that sex, exercise, and cooking were more fun and less shallow than class.

Immersed in this routine, Kep could hardly bother us. After the stress of growing up during his violent years, we were more comfortable with a bunch of him moping around our living room watching our TV than trying to fight with him. At first, it was a little difficult on Sunday afternoons, when the two of us were naked in bed, sharing our bodies and a bottle of wine, to have Keps show up dripping special sauce from their hamburgers and nuggets. This especially annoyed Tasha, who is a vegetarian. Meditative breathing techniques helped us relax. The odd thing was that Kep appeared to notice how it pained Tasha to see him eating the mass-produced beef, and he backed hisselves away through the doorframe, waiting until she was asleep to peek through the thin sliver between the hinges for the rest of the night.

The year grew into a warm spring where Kep's presence was no worse than walking by any other eyesore. Hisselves were a row of standing advertisements that could be ignored as you passed through the parking lot. Tasha was practicing to get a license in massage therapy, and I took on a few more hours at work to float us through while she studied. There was still time for our quiet Sundays. Kep stopped eating meat in our bedroom, opting for just a bun stuffed with iceberg lettuce and sauce. When we began making love he stepped outside again, practicing crowd control to get the rest of hisselves back and away from the door. We were thankful for this uncharacteristic behavior, yet for some reason it attracted even more crowds of Keps than usual. We had over twenty coming over each week. I asked a friend at work how many Keps he had at his apartment and he said they'd been increasing at his place, too, and were really nosy about his interactions with his boyfriend. He said he thought it was because they were gay. I told him that they watched Tasha and I too, and that hisselves were just getting nosier all over.

"Kep's watching James and his boyfriend, too," I told Tasha that night.

"Why does Kep want to watch us in bed?" Tasha would exclaim in frustration. "He's everywhere right? He could invade the set of some psycho porn movie, watch starlets who do ass acrobatics. We're just an everyday couple."

"Do you think we're everyday?"

"Well, to a guy like Kep we would be."

"What do you mean? Nobody really knows Kep."

"Didn't you take Kep studies back in high school? He worked at Bunny Burgers at an old mega mall, his father was a suicide, his mother in jail. He was into live action vampire games because he said D&D was too boring. He's not our aesthetic, and we're not his."

Shortly after this, I came home late from work to find a commotion of Keps in our kitchen. I pushed through them to where they had Tasha strapped to a chair amid the shards of a broken light bulb and arms and legs of Kep-multiple. By the blue glow of all four gas burners flaming simultaneously, I saw Kep leaning over Tasha, forcing links of sausage into her mouth.

I pounced on him, thrashing and pummeling with every intention of breaking bones and destroying organs. None of the other of hisselves tried to stop me. Kep fell to the floor, bleeding over a string of sausages. "Tash, he didn't hurt you, right? You're okay, right? Are you okay?" I turned raging to the other Keps. "Get out! I swear I'll kill every one of you, get out!" They hurriedly cleaned up the Kep-multiple from the kitchen floor and left me holding Tasha as she brought up semi-digested sausages in the sink.

"I fought them but they kept coming," she said. "I killed them and they pressed and pressed until they tied me up. Nothing makes any difference with Kep. I'm afraid he's going to come for us when we're alone. It's going to be worse, something worse than sausage."

**

"The Kep Council is intervening to make a special announcement," said the newscaster. It had been about a week since the sausage incident. It was around 11:30 at night, Kep had just left, and we were about to shut off the TV. A tired, gray-haired politician cleared his throat. "The Kep decades have been some of the most difficult years in the history of our nation and of our planet. Although violence has ceased since the days of the Kep Conflict, our underlying fears and concerns have never abated. Few of us are fooled by his outward passivity. The Kep Council wishes to remind everyone that we are the governmental body formed to resist Kep, to take the control of our lives and our futures away from him, and to restore the sovereignty of representative democracy." At this point, some Keps came into the camera's view and sat down next to the politician. One of them was taking notes. "You see, there has been a change in his activities of late. Although he still hasn't said a word since his rise to, um, power, he has, ah, been exhibiting some new behaviors. Writing things down for instance." The politician pointed at the Kep who was scrawling notes. "This is, um, new. And we believe it ..."

A voice sounded from behind the camera, "Can you hurry up? The Keps are packin' into the studio."

"Right. Well, Kep has informed us through a note that there will be a change. Starting tomorrow. He wrote that he has developed a new ability, something he has worked on since the beginning. He claims the whole world is going to change. We are doing everything within our power to find out what it is and if possible prevent ..."

Tasha shut off the TV. I followed her into the bedroom and turned off the lights. Those of us who grew up in the Kep decades knew there was nothing we could do about it. We, at least, weren't going to spend any more time listening to someone tell lies.

***

The next morning welcomed the sunlight of early summer. Warm with energy, we woke in a state of good-weather bliss. Anticipating heat, we brewed a collection of teabags for a batch of iced tea. We were well past the day's initial kiss when we noticed.

Kep was gone.

I ran onto the front porch, expecting a crowd of Keps locked out and too polite to break down the door. There were none.

Our neighbors were in the street, on the sidewalk, opening trash cans, looking everywhere for the Keps we expected would appear at any second.

"April Fools' Day was two months ago," I said.

Usually, people at least glared at my bad jokes, but everyone continued matter-of-factly searching for Kep. I picked up a newspaper and went inside to the TV. There were headlines about Kep's announcement, and some speculative discussions on the major networks, but through it all it was apparent that nobody thought he had truly left.

Maybe we had grown so used to Kep's presence we knew that it was still there, even though his body wasn't. It was an easy leap for me and Tasha to make, taking ambiguous terms like "energy" and "chi" on faith. Still, even the scientific and military types were staying quiet about Kep's disappearance. It was unanimous among the people that the question was not, "Is Kep really gone?" but "Where is Kep now?"

"It's unnerving, isn't it?" I said to Tasha as I went back into the kitchen. "At least we won't have a crowd at our door while we're in bed."

Tasha was staring into the decanter of iced tea, pouring in sugar, stopping, looking into the spout, then pouring in more.

"I thought you quit that stuff," I said.

Tasha turned around, staring at me blankly, then poured in another mound of sugar. "Let's drink iced tea today," she said.

"Yeah, that's why we made it."

"Let's drink iced tea," she repeated, going into the living room and plopping on the couch. She picked up the remote and switched from the news to a rerun of *Jeopardy*. She grinned and her eyes went glazed. "Hey, they have a mythology category, you should come in here."

"I just have to go to the bathroom," I said, and scurried down the hallway. She's in a strange mood, I thought. It made no sense —until I opened the bathroom door. There we were, Tasha and I. Except it wasn't me, because I was standing in the doorway and another Me was sitting on the toilet reading a pornographic comic book called *Willow the Pussy*. Tasha was leaning over me, speaking tersely, "I don't know which is worse, that you're ignoring me or that you're reading that elementary-school smut."

The Me on the toilet pointed at a round-eyed, spread-eagle cartoon angel and said, "No, you'd like this, it's actually empowering for women, you have to read it."

"Tasha!" I cried.

She turned to me, and we grasped each other. We were both cold and shaking, remembering that first feeling we had when we were kids, when the Keps came and changed everything and there was nothing we could do about it. It was changing again, infecting us ... whoever we were, since now there were four of us—the Kep-us, and the us-us.

The Kep Council disintegrated soon after. Nobody was interested in keeping track anymore. People grew fatigued. The images of Kep left and were replaced with his indeterminate doubles. Some of the politicians and generals were happy with what they thought was a restoration of power and self determination. They failed to make any distinction between which selves would be doing the determining.

Some days, I came home from work exhausted with the difficulties of dealing with my co-workers' Kep-selves. I tried to talk to Tasha about it, and I'd find her eating chocolate bars, stinking of hair spray, and watching a game show. She would lay into me for playing loud music and video games all day in my room.

We quickly lost track of who was interacting with whom, never knowing whether it was the real one of us, or a version of Kep. Sometimes, our real selves ran into each other; at random times during the weekend, we'd catch an occasional movie or do some Tai Chi. But it often degenerated into a Kep conflict where I was accused of cooking hamburgers in her tofu pan, or I thought she had sprayed the whole apartment with something toxic.

The worst thing about it was that I found myself defending my Kep-self sometimes. It made sense that he was into what he was into; he was making progress in his own way, and there was nothing really wrong with porno comics. Tasha agreed with that, as long as it wasn't in her face.

But we were in each other's faces—her hair and bug spray in mine, and my heavy metal, armpits, and porno in hers. We tried to acknowledge that it was Kep who was knocking things off balance, yet we were both worried. I wasn't sure I remembered our balance in the first place, or why it was any better. Eventually, it almost wasn't even my business to worry, because maybe I wasn't me, but the Kep-me. Let that other guy worry about it, I thought, and turned up the volume on the stereo until I couldn't hear Tasha's complaints anymore. It wasn't as mean as it sounds, since the Kep-Tasha was equally annoying with her habits. We went on living like this, our cruel habits always having the same effect in the Empire of One. Maybe we thought that someday our real selves would return to each other again. Keeping that thought, we kept on; I kept her, and she kept me.

We All Scream For Ice Cream

by MIKE SEGRETTO

"Wow," Donnie grunted, "She sure is something."

"I'll say," Dick agreed. "What I wouldn't give to have a crack at her."

Georgie Jr. shifted his butt from left to right in a futile attempt to get comfortable on the searing black-top roof.

"Hey guys," he mumbled in his slow drawl, "How long is we gonna sit up here and watch her? This sun is makin' me sleepy as a church mouse."

Georgie Jr.'s comment didn't register with his two friends because they were so caught up in watching Peepa sunbathe in the yard on the other side of the fence. Every summer since they started to take notice of girls, the boys would perch on the roof outside of Georgie Jr.'s bedroom window and watch Peepa on those days that were hot enough to soak in the sun. Today was certainly one of those days—the hottest all summer, despite the fact that summer was practically over. Well, at least it was over as far as the boys were concerned since the following Monday was Labor Day and they'd have to be back in class the following day.

"Man, oh, man." Donnie wrung his hands together. "She gets prettier and prettier every year. Her body sure didn't look like that last summer."

"Uhh huh," Dick agreed, half listening and half allowing his mind to wander. Ever since his 11th birthday, he'd been feeling differently about girls. He'd always liked them and could tell the pretty ones from the dogs, but they'd never made him feel like this before. Peepa sure was a pretty one, with her silky black hair, exotically dark skin, and almond-shaped, green eyes. There sure weren't any girls like that on Homeland Street.

"Whatever," Georgie Jr. grumbled.

From somewhere in the distance, but not the far distance, a tinkling, dissonant song drifted over the yards and trees and picket fences on an anomalous cool breeze.

"Hey, fellas," Georgie Jr. whispered. "Ya hear that?"

"Huh?" Dick only barely stirred from his reverie.

"Ice cream man," Georgie Jr. smiled.

"So what?" Dick barked.

"We should get some."

Peepa opened her eyes, still not noticing the boys watching her from the roof. She leaned over next to her lounge, picked up a small bottle of baby oil, squirted a dollop of it into her palm, and began to rub it on her back.

"Oh, man!" Donnie exclaimed as loud as he could without drawing any unwanted attention to himself. "She's gonna roll over! You know what that means, don't you?"

"Butt," Dick muttered.

"Bingo!"

"Aww, forget about butt." Georgie Jr. attempted a regal expression and declared, "Ice cream is a way for a boys to celeberate the finalizing days of the summer."

"What?" Dick puzzled. "What the hell is that? Is that English?"

"I want some ice cream, and what Georgie Jr. wants, Georgie Jr. gets! Come on." Georgie Jr. stood up and headed for his bedroom window.

Dick and Donnie sneered as Peepa turned over on her lounge, revealing her nicely developing derriére. But Georgie Jr. was right. He may not have been the brightest kid in school—hell, he may have flunked every subject the previous year—but he did always get his way. That's what happens when your daddy is the wealthiest man in town.

The boys moped downstairs and out the front door to the sidewalk. Homeland Street was as empty as can be. Aside from the still distant strains of the ice cream man's siren song, the only other sound was that of a lawn sprinkler tittering across the street.

"Okay, smart guy, where's Sadie?" Dick was still sore about leaving his peak peep position on the roof so soon.

"He's gotta be down the block. Can't you hear the music?" Georgie Jr. drawled.

"What am I, hard of hearing? I can hear the music, but I don't see his truck anywhere. Do you?"

Georgie Jr. smiled. "He's comin'. Let's take a walk down the street. I bet we find him just in time."

The boys slowly made their way down Homeland Street, trying desperately to focus on the cool, refreshing ice cream rather than the oppressive, deadening, late summer heat. September was the worst time of the summer because it was hot and humid as could be, but there was nothing left to look forward to except for another year of school, and if there was one thing the boys hated, that was books and learning and teachers. And if Georgie Jr. hated one thing more than any other thing in the whole, wide world that was being told what to do by a teacher.

"Jesus," Dick grunted. "Where the hell is Sadie?"

"Don't take the lord's name in vain," Georgie Jr. growled. "That sand nigger's gotta be around here somewhere."

"What did you call him?" Donnie asked.

"Ahh, it's just somethin' I heard my daddy call Sadie."

"Hey, Georgie," Donnie said. "What exactly happened between your old man and Sadie?"

Georgie Jr. grimaced and mopped the sweat from his face with the bottom of his tank top. "You know how Ira is always givin' me a tough time at school? Well, a few summers ago, Daddy went over to his house to talk to Sadie about it, and to told him to tell his kid to leave me alone. Sadie didn't wanna talk, so Daddy let him have one."

"You mean your Daddy hit Sadie? He hit the damn ice cream man?" Donnie asked.

"That's what Daddy said. I'll tell y'all, I ain't lookin' forward to seein' that big bully Ira back at school on Tuesday."

"Why is that kid such a big bully?" Donnie wondered as the music from the ice cream truck drew nearer. "Well," Georgie Jr. brought his voice down to confidential tones. "Daddy says that Sadie beats on Ira somethin' awful. Beats on Peepa even more."

"That son of a bitch!" Donnie cried. "Who'd beat on a hot chick like that?"

"Ira beats on her, too."

"Ha!" Dick slapped Georgie Jr. on the back. "You're lucky the oaf didn't catch you peepin' at his sister today! He wouldn't have waited till Tuesday to clobber you, let me tell you!" Georgie Jr. thought real hard for a second. He started to get a little worried, because maybe Ira was watching him and his friends from behind a curtain in his house or something. But then he relaxed. "Wait a minute. I wasn't peepin' on Peepa. You guys were."

"But you were sitting right up there with us, you dummy," Dick laughed.

"Oh, man," Georgie Jr. murmured. "You think he sawed me?"

"Yeah, Georgie," Dick chortled. "I bet he's looking to kick your ass right now."

"Oh, man."

"You know," Donnie began as the boys came to the end of Homeland Street, "it sure does stink that we gotta go to a jerk like Sadie to get ice cream."

"But I love ice cream!" Georgie Jr. cried.

"Jeez!" Dick was becoming exasperated with his dim friend. "Your dad punched the guy in the face, for Christ's sake!"

"What I tell you about the lord's name?" Georgie Jr. snapped.

Donnie continued, while the ice cream truck's music grew even louder. "All I'm saying is that I wish we had our own damn ice cream truck, and we didn't have to go buy it from a crumb like Sadie."

"That's a hell of a dream, Donnie," Dick sneered. "But I think we're gonna have to settle for buying our ice cream from Sadie for now. In fact, there he is."

Just around the corner on Q Street, Sadie's truck was parked at the mouth of the block. Standing in the window of his truck, with an expansive smile stretching below his thick, black moustache, Sadie seemed to have been waiting for the boys to arrive.

"Hello, boys!" Sadie's heavily accented tones were as unctuous as a vat of motor oil. He looked a lot older than he did a few summers ago, and his brow was drenched in thick, salty sweat droplets that glowed against his swarthy skin. "What I get for you fellows on such a hot summer day?"

"Dark chocolate!" Dick said.

"Rocky Road!" Donnie said.

"Napolean!" Georgie Jr. said.

"Napolean?" Sadie asked.

"You know, the ice cream with the vanilla, the chocolate, and the strawberry, though you can leave off the strawberry, 'cause it's pink, and pink is kinda faggy."

"Ahh," Sadie laughed. "You mean Neapolitan. Coming right up, boys." Sadie turned around slowly, paused to catch his breath, and swung open the door of the freezer box. An icy apparition floated from the box and drifted around his face. Sadie lingered for as long as he could, allowing the frigid fog to provide his weary head with some much needed refreshment. Then he reached in and pulled out three ice cream cones as a magician pulls a rabbit from a hat. Sadie spun on his heels and held the cones against his chest.

"Five dollars each, boys."

Dick's face crunched up into a contorted grimace. "Five dollars? I don't have any five dollars. Who do you think you're talking to? Donald Trump?"

Donnie and Georgie Jr. foraged through their pockets. Donnie had a dollar in loose change. Georgie Jr. could only come up with eleven cents. The sun throbbed mercilessly from above, and the humidity coiled around Georgie Jr.'s body like a boa constrictor. He wanted his ice cream.

"Five dollars, my rump!" Georgie Jr. spat. "I want my ice cream! Give it to me, you sand nigger!"

"Sand nigger, am I?" Sadie's smile disappeared as he peered closer at Georgie Jr. "I know you. You the son of that white devil with the bald head and the glasses. That wimp on Homeland Street."

Georgie Jr.'s face turned as red as a radish and his fingers clenched into little, balled-up fists. "My Daddy is not a wimp! He beat you up and he'll do it again, Sand Nigger! Sand Nigger, Sand Nigger, Sand Nigger! Give me my ice cream!"

"I give you your ice cream in hell, boy!" Sadie's brown face flooded with an eggplant hue. "You get no ice cream from Sadie today! I laugh at you!"

And Sadie laughed and laughed and laughed. And Georgie Jr.'s face turned redder and redder and redder. And Sadie's eggplant-colored face turned brighter and brighter and brighter. Through his thundering rounds of laughter, he began to cough and wheeze.

"I ... laugh ... at ... you." Sadie's choked out his words and clutched his chest with one hand, while supporting himself on the window with the other one.

"Laugh ... at ..."

Sadie keeled over in his place, his body disappearing below the truck's window and slumping to the ground.

"Sadie?" Georgie Jr. whispered. "Sadie?" He stood on his tippy toes, trying to see into the truck's window.

"Forget this junk," Donnie growled as he marched right into the truck. Sadie was lying on the floor with three scoops of ice cream melting in a muddy puddle on his chest. The three cones stood erect, jutting from his body like swords from the carcass of a slain bull.

"Holy cow!" Georgie Jr. exclaimed, while pulling himself up into the truck. "Is he?"

"Step aside," Dick snapped, shoving Georgie Jr. aside and heading straight for the freezer. "Think I can find a Nutty Buddy in here?"

Georgie Jr. trotted over to Dick's side. The boys rummaged through the freezer, filling their arms with as much ice cream as they could gather. "Looks like we hit the jackpot, Dickie boy!"

"Shut up, bonehead!" Dick mumbled as he continued filling his arms with Rocket Pops and Cherry Bombs. Georgie Jr. was so wrapped up in compiling his own stash of booty that he didn't pay much notice to Dick's barb, nor did he notice Donnie trotting past him to the front of the truck.

"Hmmm, now I've seen my dad do this a million, billion times," Donnie muttered. He turned the key of the truck and the engine sputtered into action. Then he jerked back the gearshift. The truck lurched forward, momentarily knocking Dick and Georgie Jr. off their feet.

"What the hell are you doing?" Dick shouted.

"Making the dream come true!" Donnie yelled. "Now get me a damn Mickey Mouse bar!"

Dick broke into hysterical laughter and rushed to his friend in the front of the truck with his arms loaded with frozen treats. The truck swerved wildly round the corner and back down Homeland Street. Georgie Jr. stuffed his face with every sweet he could get his hands on, and his brain buzzed and burst to life with wave after wave of sugar-tweaked endorphins. He too was laughing maniacal-ly now.

"I can't believe we're doin' this!" Georgie Jr. exclaimed. "We got our very own ice cream truck and all the ice cream to us-selves!"

Donnie curtly slammed on the breaks. "Wait a minute, guys." Georgie Jr. and Dick froze, not even swallowing the gobs of half-chewed ice cream in their stuffed mouths. "Maybe we should give some of this ice cream to the other kids in the neighborhood." Georgie Jr. and Dick couldn't believe their ears, and they did not move an inch.

"Just joking. Ha ha ha ha ha!!"

Georgie Jr. and Dick dropped to the floor and rolled from side to side, unable to control the girlish giggles and gut wrenching guf-faws that flowed out of them. Georgie Jr. did his best to stifle the laughter by shoving more ice cream into his mouth, but he could not snuff out his joy. "I can't believe we're doing this!" His words were barely decipherable through the wad of ice cream.

"Hmmm," Donnie scratched his chin. "I'll tell you who probably would like some of this ice cream. And who knows how she'd show her thanks if she knew that, we don't just have all the ice cream she can eat, but we also have her dead daddy riding shotgun with us. That's the last time he's gonna rough up Peepa!"

Dick's face became serious and controlled. "Yeah. Yeah, head back down Q Street. Let's swing by Peepa's place. I bet she's still laying on her stomach. What I wouldn't do to get another glimpse of that butt."

Donnie made a screeching U-turn and barreled back to Q Street. The truck swerved down the block, and the boys laughed at the expression of an incredulous driver, who couldn't believe her eyes when she got a load of the careening ice cream truck piloted by three lads that was heading straight for her. To avoid a collision, the woman drove her car up on the closest lawn she could reach.

"Yee haw!' Georgie Jr. howled. "That was a close 'un!"

Donnie stopped the truck again. He looked over his shoulder nervously, expecting the woman to make a swift 911 call on her cell phone and report the boys for causing such mayhem. But she didn't. She simply restarted her car and continued back down Homeland Street, appearing smaller and smaller until she disappeared in the far distance.

"Ha!" Georgie Jr. hiccupped smugly. "She must've seen the son of the richest daddy in town and thought best to keep her lip buttoned. I can't believe we're gettin' away with this!"

"Who cares about that woman, that maggot!" Dick screamed. "We're on a mission here!"

Donnie started the truck up again, driving more madly than ever. All he and Dick could think about was Peepa's body glistening in the sweltering summer sun. They bet there was nothing a girl like that wanted more than a cool, refreshing cone.

Donnie sped the vehicle on down Q Street, further and further until he saw a familiar form huddled on the walk in front of a familiar house at the far end of the block.

"What the hell is that psycho doing?" Dick barked.

Ira was crouching near the curb, holding a magnifying glass over a large mound of sand that rose from between two bricks in the sidewalk. As Ira looked down with intense concentration, tiny ants combusted under the sun rays intensified through his magnifying glass.

"What a psycho!" Donnie mused.

"Well," Georgie Jr. declared, "that Bully done killed his lastest ant!"

Georgie Jr. grabbed the steering wheel and stomped his foot down over Donnie's, pressing the gas pedal right down to the floor. The tires shrieked. The ice cream truck, still blaring its off-key, jingling, summer tune, skidded down the street, straight into Ira.

Donnie slammed on the brakes. "Now you've done it, Georgie!" He sprang out of his seat and out the door of the truck. Donnie threw his hands over his gaping maw. "What did you do, Georgie?"

Georgie Jr. followed Donnie out of the truck. He stepped to the front of the vehicle. The grill was smashed and chunks of flesh cooked between the slats. No trace of Ira's body remained on the sidewalk. Georgie Jr. dropped to his knees and inspected the underside of the truck, where he saw more seared hunks of flesh stuck to the overheated undercarriage. He stood back up and looked down the block.

"It don't matter." Georgie Jr. eyes were ablaze with madness. "It don't matter. No one saw nothin', no one's gonna say nothin'. We're gettin' away with it. We're gettin' away with it." Georgie Jr.

produced an Eskimo Pie from out of nowhere and bit into it. The sugar went straight to his head and filled him with the immeasurable sense that he was indestructible.

"Shut up! Shut up!" Dick screamed. "Get in here! We're on a mission!"

Dick felt something that he'd never felt before. It was a burning sensation that began in his waist and continued down his thighs. He kind of felt like he had to pee, but he knew that going to the bathroom wouldn't relieve the throbbing sensation. As soon as Georgie Jr. and Donnie rushed back into the truck, Dick thrust his foot on the gas pedal and crashed the vehicle straight through the fence alongside the house. The truck lumbered into the yard, where Peepa was, indeed, still sunbathing. She held her hands over herself in a pathetic attempt to cover her flesh. Her eyes darted around the yard, but it was completely enclosed—a fence behind her and a mammoth ice cream truck before her.

"I bet she'd like some ice cream," Donnie mumbled.

"Fuck the ice cream," Dick growled.

"I can't believe we're gettin' away with this," Georgie Jr. smiled.

A Man's Gotta Eat What a Man's Gotta Eat

by DANA FREDSTI

The name's T-Bone. Chuck T-Bone. I'm a private detective. You know, a P. I., a dick, a gumshoe. To be specific, I find missing people. It's always been my specialty, even before the big change. After I died, I changed my name to fit my new life—though 'life' might not be the right word under the circumstances.

Back in the old days, I was Charles Tyrone of Tyrone's Investigative Services. But I bought it while doing a job for a promi-nent family—an Italian family with connections in all the wrong places. They paid me well, and I've never had enough money to be choosy about who I worked for. I've always tried to stay on the clean side of the law, but it ain't easy, even these days.

***

Yeah, I'm a zombie. Undead, living dead, ghoul—take your pick. I say we're just ordinary guys and dolls trying to earn an honest day's wages and put food on the table, same way we did before this zombie crap really started to hit the fan. You know, back a year or so when the dead starting refusing to stay buried. Having corpses walking around in various states of decay was bad enough, but then it became obvious that the dead's favorite pastime was chowing down on the living. You'd step outside of your house and bam! Instant corpse kibble.

It was Wednesday morning, the middle of a hot July week. Smog lay over the San Fernando Valley in a thick haze and it was hotter than the Sahara outside. I was kicking back in my office, air conditioner cranked to the max, as I waited for a new case to keep me in grub and pay the bills. Used to be that J.D. took up most of my pay, but now I only drink it out of habit. These days it was more important to pay the bills, especially the electricity so you could keep your home and your workspace nice and frosty. Dead meat rots if you don't keep it cold. I was still in pretty good shape after six months. A little green around the gills, maybe, but nothing major. One of these days I was gonna go down to one of the local mortuary joints and get myself embalmed. But that took more do-re-mi than I had to spare, so in the meantime I'd make due with my J.D. I figure my insides must be fairly pickled as is.

It had started out to be a slow week, and so far there were no signs of things getting on the speed track. My bank account was flatter than a ten year old in a training bra, and if something didn't break soon, I was gonna join the lines at the unemployment office.

I was just starting to sink into a depression darker than an African night when the door opened and she walked in. She didn't knock, but then trouble rarely waits to be invited. Tall and still lusciously curved, she swayed towards me. This could've been on account of the fact that her dainty feet were encased in black stiletto heels, the kind that said, "Fuck me, but don't ask me to walk." Nice gams, kind of slender, so slender that in a couple of places I could see bone showing beneath the seamed stockings.

Her hair, where it still clung to her scalp, was blonde and luxuriant. Heavy makeup gave her once porcelain, now bluish, complexion an almost natural skin tone, marred only by a gash across one cheek that no expensive mortician's putty could hide. Her nails were painted red to match her lipstick and her low-necked, curve-clinging satin dress. A black silk scarf draped around her throat and shoulders didn't quite conceal the gaping wound where someone had given her the King Kong of hickeys right above the collarbone. Her peepers were still an icy blue, but Brother, all the Visine in the world couldn't get the red out. All in all, I wouldn't kick her out of my bed.

"So, what can I do for you, Miss ..."

I paused, waiting for her to fill in the blank.

"Gionetti. *Mrs.* Robert Gionetti." She watched me closely as she gave her name, as if expecting some kind of reaction.

I reacted all right, but only on the inside. A good P.I. never gives anything away.

She seemed disappointed. "Don't you recognize the name?"

"I don't know," I replied coolly. "Should I?"

Her tone became caustic. "Perhaps you've been dead a little longer than we'd thought."

I shrugged. "Maybe there's some people a man would rather forget."

"Like this one?" Mrs. Gionetti opened her small black handbag, pulled out a slightly yellowed photo, and held it out to me. I took it, lifting my feet from the desk and swiveling my chair around so that my back was to her. It was a good thing I did, because seeing the photo hit me like a gut punch and I had a hunch Mrs. Gionetti would've enjoyed it.

"Well?" Mrs. G. sounded faintly triumphant. "Does that ring any bells?"

I made sure my voice was carefully neutral. "Yeah, as a matter of fact. Quite a few."

"I thought it might."

Her smug tone was really beginning to piss me off. I turned back towards her and flipped the picture face down on the desk.

"This is old business," I said. "Why bring it up now?"

Mrs. Gionetti smiled, causing the gash in her cheek to crack open a little more. "On the contrary, Mr. T-Bone. This is unfinished business. I believe you were killed before completing the job that my family originally hired you to do. Very sloppy work."

That hurt. "Yeah?" I snarled. "Well, it doesn't look like your family lasted much longer than I did, sister. And at least I had a clean death. You didn't see me ending up as boxed lunch for a zombie."

I could tell I'd struck home when she raised one hand to her wounded cheek. Her face would've been flushed with anger if her arterial ketchup still circulated.

"How dare you! I was with my husband when he died and ..."

"And the first thing he said when he got back up was 'Gee, honey, you look good enough to eat!'"

I grabbed her wrist as she sprang to her feet and tried to slap me from across the desk. "I wouldn't do that," I cautioned as she tugged angrily against my grip. "You might lose your hand."

She immediately stopped struggling. I let go of her wrist and she sat back down. I gave her a few minutes to regain her composure and thought about how many people were offed because of sentimentality. I mean, the first thing most newly dead folk did after rising was hightail it to their homes or workplaces, depending on where they spent the most time while alive. So, you have your basic schmoe, who should be under a slab of granite, and instead he's walking in the front door of his house, nothing on his mind but 'what's for dinner.' Who should be there but the little woman and maybe a couple of brats. So, what does his grieving widow do? Does she go for a gun or even a baseball bat? Nope. Nine times out of ten, the dumb broad would scream "Darling!" and run right into the arms of her hungry hubby. And dinner is served. Hubby'd have his meal, wife would come back minus a few pieces, a little kid a la mode for dessert ... And, yeah, there were guys who made the same mistake, but it really strikes me as being a female kind of thing. Mrs. G., here, seemed to be a prime example.

"So," I said casually. "The Gionettis have unfinished business they want wrapped up?"

"That is correct, Mr. T-Bone." Mrs. G.'s voice dripped icicles.

"And you want me to finish what I started."

"Yes. And as before, the authorities are not to be involved."

"Withholding live meat for the purpose of private consumption is highly illegal."

"We're aware of that, Mr. T-Bone. We'll make it worth the risk."

"My fees have gone up. Cost of not living and all that."

"Money is no object."

"I didn't think it would be."

Mrs. Gionetti took an envelope out of her purse and laid it on the desk. "You'll find ten thousand in the envelope. That should be an adequate advance against any expenses you might incur." She stood up and turned to leave.

"There's just one other thing," I said.

She stopped, teetering precariously on her heels as she snapped impatiently, "What is it?"

"I'm just curious. What difference could this possibly make to the Gionettis now?"

Mrs. Gionetti looked at me. "We believe in paying our debts, Mr. T-Bone. And that other people should pay theirs, as well. We see no reason why death should change that. Good day."

I watched appreciatively as she swayed out the door, her rounded ass clearly defined beneath the satin of her dress.

Mrs. G. was right about one thing—death really didn't change things a hell of a lot. So you died. After the initial rigor mortis wore off, you started getting your smarts back. It took a couple of days and some zombies were still damned stupid, but sooner or later most of us were able to function as well as we did before we died, going back to our old professions. Yup, the only things that had really changed were our diets. No such thing as vegetarians any more.

I shook my head in disgust. Here I was with a job to do and I was wasting my time on zombie philosophy.

I picked up the photo that was still face down on my desk. One thing that definitely hadn't changed was the flip-flop of my stomach when I looked at the girl in the picture.

Lana Malloy, former love of my life and the cause of my death. She'd been something all right, a curvy brunette with big blue eyes and full, pouting lips that were made for kissing. Her breasts were like firm summer melons and she had the kind of round ass that you wanted to sink your teeth into...no pun intended.

Lana had been the girlfriend of Marco Gionetti, the middle son of Don Roberto Gionetti, Mafia don. Somehow Lana had gotten a hold of a shipment of gold belonging to the Family and had then taken a powder with the dough. So, they wanted the dame found, preferably alive, so they could have some fun before altering that state. They didn't care that the world was going to hell around them, it was still business as usual.

It hadn't taken me long to find her. Like I said, finding people has always been my specialty. Lana was hiding out with an old roommate. She and said roommate had both worked Hollywood

Boulevard before Lana had been spotted by Marco. Her roommate now worked out of a seedy hotel seeing how it wasn't safe to work the streets any more.

I found Lana at the hotel. She was alone, an easy target. All I had to do was deliver her to the Gionettis, collect my dough and buy myself a case of J.D. to celebrate. But no, I had to be a sap and fall for her. She knew what I was there for, all right, and fed me a sob story about how she'd been forced to steal the gold for Marco, who was in on the heist from jump street, her failed career as an actress, the whole nine yards. And I fell for it, hook, line and sinker, especially after she laid a lip lock on me that would've brought the dead back to life if the virus or radiation or whatever everyone was babbling about hadn't already done just that. This was it for me; the girl of my dreams.

We made plans to leave L.A.—not an easy task seeing how the Government was placing all major cities under quarantine. The bottom line was that having armed guards at all major routes in and out of Los Angeles made it hard for anyone who'd had enough of the laid-back Southern California lifestyle. But I'm nothing if not creative.

I called on every connection and favor that I'd collected over the years and it was long before I'd put together a fairly foolproof plan. I'd pick Lana up at the hotel at one in the a.m. We'd go to a pre-arranged location and meet a buddy of mine who'd have an armored car waiting to get us through the roadblocks and up to a little hideaway in the mountains. In the car would be enough supplies and ammo to get us through a few years. My only mistake was filling little Lana in on the details. But you know how it is when the little head takes over—common sense and good judgment go right out the window.

At any rate, the plan went as smooth as silk up to the high-rise parking lot where we were meeting my buddy Larry with the armored car. Larry was there, all right, along with the car, but so was an unwelcome third party, one Marco Gionetti. He had a .38 pointed at my pal and a shark's smile on his ugly mug. One quick look at my baby told me all I needed to know. Lana'd suckered me into doing all the dirty work just so she could hightail it out of town with Marco.

Lana sashayed over to her pasta-eating Romeo, who settled an arm across her shoulders in a way that still boiled my blood even though Lana'd double-crossed me. Marco smirked and, motioning me over by Larry, said, "Thanks for doing all the work, Tyrone. Me and Lana, we really appreciate it."

"I'll bet you do." I stared unblinkingly at Lana.

"I'm sorry, Charles," Lana said with what I'd still swear was genuine regret. "We had some good times together."

"We could have had a lot more, baby." I started to inch my hand towards my shoulder holster. At this point I figured I had nothing to lose.

"Enough sweet talk," snarled Marco. "Say good-bye to Mr. Tyrone, doll-face."

"At least let Larry go," I said, stalling for time.

"Sorry, Tyrone. I don't leave loose ends behind."

I knew I had to act fast, so I did. Whipping my .44 out of my holster, I got off a shot just as Marco pulled his trigger. White-hot agony exploded in my chest. As the world started going black, I managed to squeeze off two more shots. My only regret as I exited the world of the living was that I didn't get to see if I'd hit the bastard. I didn't have to regret for very long, though.

A couple hours later, the zombie bug kicked in and the first sight that greeted me was that of Marco Gionetti lying on the floor, one kneecap shattered and another bullet wound through his shoulder. He was groaning in agony and trying feebly to crawl to his car. I would've smiled but my muscles hadn't loosened up yet. The pain in my chest was gone and I felt pretty damned good, the only exception being a hellacious hunger. Luckily for me, I had a blue-plate special waiting for me by the name of Marco and I've always liked Italian food.

I shook my head. This little trip down memory lane was getting me nowhere but more confused. I'd never worked out my feelings for Lana and her betrayal, had tried not to think about it. But now I was being paid to find her. And I had to figure out what I'd do when I did. Would I want to kiss her or eat her?

I stared at her picture, trying to find the answer in those luscious lips, those sea-blue peepers, those perfect breasts that were so enticing … and edible.

Before long I was as frustrated as a zombie in a mannequin factory. "Aw, screw it!" I jammed the picture into my pants pocket and stood up, slamming my chair against the desk. I'd deal with my personal problems later. Right now I had a job to do. It was time to get on the speed track and start. Besides, it was lunch time and I couldn't think on an empty stomach.

First thing I did was douse myself with bug repellent. The worst thing about going outside was the damned flies. And you know what they say: where there's flies, there's maggots.

I grabbed my trench coat and fedora off the coat rack. Yeah, I know, what does a zombie need with a coat? Hey, I like the look. And my fedora did double duty. I'd had it lined with steel, so not only did it protect my slowly decaying noggin from the elements, it also took care of any stray bullets that came my way.

I left my office and hit the street. My first stop was just down the block on the corner of Laurel Canyon and Ventura Boulevard, so I figured a little smog and heat couldn't hurt. At least it was a dry heat. The zombies in Florida must really be hating life in all that humidity.

Joe's Joints was packed. The logo, a severed leg in the hands of a well-preserved California zombie gal with a wide smile on her blue face proclaimed, "One million served!" No kidding. And every single one of the goddamn million was standing in line today.

After waiting in line for a half hour for my elbow joint ("freshly killed!") with a side order of toes I decided to call a cab instead of driving to my next destination. Gas was still expensive, and parking in Hollywood is a bitch. Shortly after I placed the call, an old Yellow cab pulled up in front of Joes's. It looked like it'd seen quite a few years of duty. The same went for the Cabbie, who turned around as I settled myself in the back seat. He was an old guy, blue cap perched jauntily over one runny eye. "Where to, Mac?" His voice had gone from gravelly to gargly and there was a dark cavity where his nose had been.

"Hollywood and Vine," I instructed. "And crank up the air conditioner, will ya? Christ on a crutch, a guy could decompose just sitting in this trash heap."

"Sure, Mac," the Cabbie said agreeably. "Whatever you say, you're the fare." The muscles and tendons in his neck made ominous tearing sounds as he turned back to the wheel and peeled out into the light afternoon traffic. He hit the 'high' switch on the air conditioner and rolled up his window.

We passed Mulholland Drive and started the descent into Hollywood. Soon we were on Hollywood Boulevard, going east. Once past La Brea, activity on the street picked up. Punks, prostitutes, and the occasional tourist strolled, lurched, and crawled along the Boulevard, some looking to be discovered by some big shot movie maker, others just looking for trouble. These were the kind of scum who'd sell their mother for a plugged nickel ... if they didn't eat her first.

You saw a lot more transients on this side of the hill, a lot more missing limbs and rotting faces. These were the zombies with no place to go, no homes, no food. And with the Republicans in office, you can bet your balls that there'd be no funding available for shelters and low-income housing projects. They can bring the dead to life, but they still can't solve the homeless problem.

A couple of blocks from Vine I said, "I want you to turn on Vine and pull up to the curb. And I want you to wait for me. Got that, Pal?"

Cabbie turned onto Vine and parked. I exited the cab and headed back to Hollywood Boulevard, hanging a left at the corner. I immediately started scanning the faces—I was looking for Lana's ex-roommate, Jackie. I had a hunch she'd be back on her favorite strip of the Boulevard now that she didn't have to worry about undead johns. It was a long shot that she'd have any clue as to Lana's whereabouts, but I didn't have any better ideas at the moment.

It looked like I may have crapped out on this particular gamble. There was no sign of Jackie among the rest of the hookers and dealers leaning against poles and store fronts. Maybe it was time to use some muscle to find out where Jackie was hiding.

"Hey, handsome, looking for fun?"

The voice came from a dame in one of those black leather bra things, the type with metal studs all over it. Her filling was starting to deflate, but the legs that showed beneath the black mini were still good enough to get my Grade-A rating. She was leaning against the side window of a wig shop, her hips pushed forward as far as they'd go.

Maybe I wouldn't need muscle to find out about Jackie.

"No thanks, doll," I replied, walking over to her. "Though, I gotta say, the offer's tempting."

"C'mon," she wheedled, running a finger down my coat front. The nail fell off and we both pretended not to notice. "What've you got to lose?"

"I'm down here on business, sweetheart. But maybe you could give me a little hand."

"That's just one of the things I had in mind, honey." She gave my crotch a squeeze, not too hard though. I bet she'd lost a few prospective clients that way.

"Sorry, babe." I gently but firmly moved her hand away from my genitals. "Now how about some info?"

She pouted, clearly piqued that I wasn't interested. I knew how to pacify her. I extracted a twenty-dollar bill from my coat pocket. "This oughta buy you a nice lunch, baby. Uh uh, not so fast." I pulled the bill out of reach as her greedy little hands stretched out for it.

"What d'ya want to know?" She was all flirtatious smiles again, warmed up by the sight of cash.

"You know Jackie? Short, blonde, usually works this block?"

"Yeah, I know her. If she's not here, she's probably over at Club Dead. She hustles there when business is slow on the Boulevard."

"Over by the Ivar, right?"

She nodded, her gaze glued to the twenty. "If she ain't on the dance floor, chances are she's in the can, powdering what's left of her nose."

I handed over the dough. "Thanks, doll face."

I walked to the next block and went left, walking past the library. Club Dead was down a mini-alley next door to the strip joint, painted white with splashes of red.

It was dark and smoky inside, a band playing loudly on the small stage at the back of the place. I paid the doorman two bucks cover charge and went over to the bar.

I ordered a shot of J.D. and leaned against the bar, scanning the crowd for Jackie. The place was packed for mid-afternoon, the little dance floor a mass of bodies jerking around in time to the music. The band played with a voodoo drum beat that was kind of catchy. I mean, it wasn't the Stones or Elvis, but it was good rock and roll. And come to think of it, Mick's last album hadn't been that hot, and Elvis was *still* dead, though if someone sighted him these days, I might consider the possibility.

I checked out the women. Slim pickings for anyone wanting intellectual stimulation, but plenty for those interested in stimulation of a more physical type. Now I knew where bimbos went when they died. But all the eye candy wasn't helping me locate Jackie.

The stairs leading to the ladies room were at the far end of the cracked and peeling hall, but I didn't have to do any climbing. Just as I set my foot on the bottom stair, a door opened at the top of the landing and Jackie started down.

She came at me in sections, losing more pieces than a jigsaw puzzle with every step. By the time she'd reached the bottom, little bits of her were littering the staircase. Jackie stopped when she saw me, recognition in her eyes. I didn't trust her as far as I could throw her, and if I threw her, I didn't think there'd be much left to question. When she spoke, it was in the kind of low, throaty voice that told me her vocal cords were in the last stages of decay.

"If it ain't Charles Tyrone," she gurgled, pure dislike evident in what was left of her face. "Haven't seen you around for awhile. I liked it that way."

I was beginning to remember that Jackie and I had never hit it off. "The feeling's mutual, sister."

"Yeah? Then why don't you take a hike, Tyrone? I got work to do."

"The name's T-Bone these days, sister."

Jackie snorted and a piece of nostril fluttered to the ground.

"I ain't here for small talk. I want information and since I know you ain't gonna do anything out of love, let's just cut the crap and get down to business." I pulled a couple hundred in greenbacks out of the wad in my wallet. Her eyes widened. "All I want to know is if you've seen Lana.

I guess the sound coming out of her throat was a laugh. "You just don't know when to quit, do you, Tyrone? Lana played you for a sap and you fell for it. The happiest day of my life was when she told me she was gonna double-cross you. She was too good for a nickel and dime dick like you."

"Thanks for the support, sister." I wasn't going to let Jackie see that the reminder of Lana's betrayal still hit me like a kick in the groin. "You want the dough or not?"

"Oh, I'll take the money," said Jackie. "And I'll even tell you the truth, for all the good it'll do you. I haven't seen Lana since the night you picked her up at the hotel. And she would've come back there. I mean, even if she'd died, she would've at least come back to tell me. We was best friends."

I doubted that but didn't have the heart to say so. Jackie was as loyal as a dog to Lana, but Lana wasn't loyal to anyone but Lana.

There was no doubt that Jackie was telling the truth. And she had a point. Lana would've probably gone back to the hotel just out of convenience. It was beginning to look like she might be dead. Not undead, just plain dead.

I gave Jackie the money. I hoped she could spend it before she fell apart completely.

"Sorry I couldn't help you, Tyrone."

"Yeah." And if sarcasm was maple syrup, you could've served me up at the IHOP. "See ya, sister."

I left in a hurry. Jackie's condition made me want to get back to the air-conditioned cab before I started falling apart at the seams. As soon as this job was finished, I was going to get myself embalmed, that was it.

As I walked back to the cab, I had the feeling I was being watched. I couldn't spot anyone obvious, but when you've been in this business as long as I have, you learn to trust that sixth sense. And it would be in character for the Gionettis to put a tail on me.

The cabby was reading the *L.A. Times* in the front seat. He put the paper away when I got in the back, and started the engine.

"Where to now, Mac?"

Good question. If Lana *was* dead, I might as well head right back to my office. But something just didn't seem right.

I told the cabby to head west on Sunset and settled back to think. There was some piece of the puzzle missing, something that'd been nagging at the back of my brain ever since the night I'd been iced. But what?

Suddenly, a hunch lurched up my leg and chomped me on the ass. Larry. What had happened to Larry after Marco and I played target practice with each other? When I'd been reborn, so to speak, Larry had been gone, along with Lana and the armored car. It was hard to believe I hadn't seen the connection before now, but I guess I just didn't want to think about it.

"Take the 10 to Venice," I said. "You'll take the 4th Street exit and head south."

It took about forty minutes to get to Venice. We drove down Fourth, turned right on Rose, and parked next to the North Beach Grill, a building topped by a giant clown in a tutu. Ugliest goddamn piece of sculpture I'd ever seen. If *it* ever came to life and starting walking the streets, I'd run for the hills.

Larry lived on Paloma Avenue, one of the little walk streets that ran perpendicular to the boardwalk, in a small Cape Cod style cottage with a postage-stamp yard. Toys were scattered all over the brown grass and I could hear the shrill screams of kids at play from inside the house. I could also hear the even shriller screams of Larry's wife, Ella, telling the kids to shut up.

I rang the buzzer. It took a few minutes, but Ella finally opened the front door.

Larry'd always been a skinny guy. Ella, on the other hand, was large, at least two hundred pounds or so, and she still possessed a considerable amount of her former bulk. They'd been the original Mr. and Mrs. Spratt.

Piggy little eyes stared at me suspiciously from a face that could stop a clock back when it was pink and healthy. Now it could've taken out Big Ben. "What do you want?" she snapped.

"The name's T-Bone, Ma'am. I was a pal of Larry's."

This information didn't help diplomatic relations at all. At the mention of Larry's name, Ella's face grew even meaner, her eyes narrowing until they almost vanished into the folds of puffy blue-grey flesh that surrounded them. "Larry!" She spat out his name like it was spoiled meat. "That no-good, son-of-a-bitch! Running off and leaving me to take care of three brats, all on a waitress's salary!"

"I take it you haven't seen him lately?"

That was all it took to get Ella to spill her guts. What it boiled down to—after wading through the stream of venom that spilled out of her mouth—was that she hadn't seen Larry since (you guessed it) the night I died.

I'd found out what I needed in order to plan my next move. I hurried back to the cab, not surprised to see a dark blue sedan parked down the block, two guys in black sitting inside. I love it when these Mafia types try to be inconspicuous. I gave them a cheerful wave as I got into my cab. Giving my office address to Cabbie, I added, "Step on it." He did, losing the bozos in the sedan in no time. Yeah, they probably knew where I worked and lived, but half the fun was pissing them off.

Back in my office, I made a quick phone call to set up a rental car. I needed something that could take mountain roads at some speed and preferably something that the goons in the sedan wouldn't recognize. My instinct was working double time and it was telling me that I'd find Lana and Larry at that little mountain hideaway where I'd planned to take Lana. The one I'd told her all about.

It was dusk by the time I'd gotten my shit together and dropped off my car at the Avis rental office, but that was okay. I knew the route up into the San Bernadino mountains like the back of my hand. And zombies have great night vision, one of the many perks of being dead.

I knew I was being followed as I drove out of L.A., and I started to wonder just what the Gionettis had in mind. I wouldn't put it past them to let me do all the leg work finding Lana and then have me offed so they wouldn't have to pay the rest of my fee. I figured I'd let 'em follow, though. What the hell? If I couldn't take care of two cheap gunsels, I didn't deserve my P.I. license, expired or not.

I almost missed the turn-off in the dark. It'd been a long time since I'd been up here and the road was now overgrown with bushes and overhanging branches. It couldn't even really be called a road; it was more like a dirt track. Of course, that was the beauty of this place. If you didn't know it was here, odds were you'd never find it. Larry'd been up here with me a couple of times, drinking weekends out with the boys. Even so, I'd be impressed if he'd found the place.

About a mile up, there was another little turn-off, even narrower than the first one. I saw the headlights of my buddies in the sedan as I turned. This road wound uphill for about five miles and led to a small cabin, built back in the sixties by my old man. As far as I knew, there were no other cabins around for miles.

My guts started churning as the cabin came into view. Someone was definitely home; a light was burning in the front room. When I saw the armored car parked around the side, my innards started doing gold-medal gymnastics.

I turned the lights off and parked in front of the cabin. They had to have heard me coming up the road because I could hear the sedan and it was still a few miles back. I figured I had a couple of minutes to confront my ex-gal and pal before I had to deal with the Gionettis apemen.

Pulling my fedora firmly down on my head, I pulled out my .44 and yelled, "Hey, Larry! Come say hi to an old drinking buddy!"

I heard the sound of arguing from behind the closed door. I recognized both the voices. I wondered if they'd recognized mine.

I heard a scuffle, then a thump followed by a sharp squeak of feminine outrage. I smiled as the door slowly opened a crack and Larry said cautiously, "Charley? Is that you?

"None other, pal."

"Charley!" Larry flung the door wide open, all caution thrown to the wind. "Charley," he repeated. "This is great! We thought you were dead, but ..." Larry stopped as the light from the front room illuminated my face.

"You were right, pal." I took a step forward, kind of touched at the reception. It was nice to know who your friends were. Only now, Larry was stumbling backwards into the cabin, falling into Lana, who'd been picking herself up off the floor. I looked at her, admiring the way her jeans and sweater clung to her ample curves like a second skin. One I'd like to peel off. "Hi, baby."

"Ch ... ch ... Charles?" Lana looked as green as a year-old zombie, her gorgeous blue orbs wide with disbelief.

"It's me, doll." I stepped inside and shut the door, looking around. "Place looks great."

Both of them started babbling at once, Larry going on about how it wasn't what it looked like, Lana telling me that she'd really always loved me, Marco had made her double-cross me, etc.

"Forget it," I cut in sharply. "I'm not stupid like I was, baby, so save your breath. You needed a man to take care of you since both Marco and I were out of the show, and Larry was there." Turning to Larry, I added, "Just between you and me, pal, I can't say I blame you. Why go home to sardines when you can have caviar?"

"Why are you here?" Larry tried to sound casual, failing miserably. I guess he knew what kind of diet I was on.

"I'd like to say I'm here to chew over old times, but this is strictly business." I looked at Lana. "You know those Italians, baby. Forgive and forget just ain't their motto."

Lana turned white. "The Gionettis?" Her voice went up an octave. "You're here to find me for them?"

I couldn't believe it. This dame had led me on, gotten me killed and now she was sounding all hurt and angry that I wasn't here to kiss and make up. I started getting a little steamed myself. "Baby, you've got one hell of a nerve if you think I owe you any loyalty."

Larry cleared his throat. "Charley, you can't do this."

The sound of a car pulling up saved Larry from finding out just how much I'd changed. "If these goons have their way, I won't have to. They'll do it for me."

"Who is it?" Lana clutched Larry's arm as I switched off the light and moved to the window, gun held ready.

"Just another double-cross in the making, baby. But this time I'm ready for it."

I opened the window as the two thugs got out of the car. Both of them were blue and ugly.

"You guys lost?"

They both whirled towards the window, guns out.

"That you, T-Bone?" I noticed the goon that spoke didn't put his gun away. I stood tense, poised for action.

"That's me," I replied, staying to the side of the window. "But you're one up on me. I don't know who the hell you are and if you don't give me a real good reason for tailgating me all day, I'm gonna ventilate your brains. My guess is that you're working for Don Roberto."

"Good guess," said the other gunsel in an attempt at joviality that was as fake as paste diamonds. "The Gionettis, they wanted to make sure you don't have any trouble, see?"

"Yeah? That's real nice. How come I don't believe you?"

"Aw, hey, T-Bone," said the first one. "You know the Gionettis don't welch on their deals."

"Yeah, but they might just hold the fact that I ate one of their relatives against me."

"You ate Marco?" This was Lana. She sounded like she was gonna toss her pancakes.

"Now if you punks were to put your pieces on the ground and step away, I might believe you're on the level. And in case your night vision ain't so great, I got my gun aimed right at your heads."

"Yeah, sure, T-Bone. No problem."

Both stooped towards the ground, guns held by the barrel. For a brief moment I thought they might actually be playing it straight with me.

Suddenly, one of the gunsels dived to the side, flipping his gun around and firing in one neat motion. The bullet shattered the window.

Lana screamed.

At the same time, the other goon did an awkward roll that had to jar the bones. I fired, missing as I ducked his bullet. I fired again as he stumbled to his feet, this time hitting him in the shoulder. He reeled backwards from the impact. I took advantage of the moment and shot him cleanly through the head. He crumpled to the ground, finally ready to try on halos.

Another scream from Lana alerted me to the fact that while I was dusting his pal, the first goon had made through the front door. He fired before I could take cover, the bullet smashing me in the forehead and knocking me flat on my back.

I heard Larry yell, "Charley!" and start towards me. The thug fired again, and there was a loud *thump* as Larry fell to the floor.

Lana shrieked again, but stayed where she was.

I lay still, eyes closed, a firm grip on my gun. My would-be killer walked over and stood above my body, no doubt gloating. I gave him a few seconds to have his fun and then opened my eyes and sat up.

It was great. He looked like he'd seen a ghost. I mean, the dead coming back to life was an everyday occurrence, but how often does a zombie come back a second time around?

"Sucker," I said, and blew his brains out.

I took off my fedora and inspected the damage. Scorch marks and a nice little hole in the felt. The steel dented in a bit at the point of impact and I supposed I'd have a corresponding dent in my head, but oh well. Life's a bitch, ain't it?

As I put my hat back on, I heard a groan and remembered Larry. Larry, who'd gotten shot because of me.

I went over to where my old pal lay in an expanding pool of blood. The bullet had taken him through the chest and there was no doubt that he was dying.

"Hey, pal." I put a hand on his shoulder.

Larry's eyes opened and he tried to focus. "Charley?" His voice was weak.

"Yeah. I'm here, pal."

One hand went up to pat mine. "It was good to see you again, Charley ... even ... if you are kind of ... of ... dead." His hand slid off limply and his eyes glazed over. I felt for his pulse. Nada.

I was silent for a moment in respect for a true pal.

Then I stood up and turned to Lana.

She was backed into a corner, hands clutching the wall as if it'd protect her. Her breasts heaved against the tight fabric of her shirt as she stared at me in terror. She was delectable.

"You ... you're not really going to take me back to the Gionettis, are you, Charles?" Lana's voice quavered, a note of desperate appeal running through it.

I looked at her and considered my options.

One, I could turn her over to the Gionettis for fun and games, but after the crap they tried to pull, I wasn't about to give them the satisfaction.

Two, I could give Lana a quick bullet through the heart and we could take up where we'd left off. But I knew I'd never really be able to trust her. And somehow, I didn't think I could stand to watch the inevitable decay of her beauty. Sooner or later those sapphire eyes would sink into blackened flesh, those perfect breasts would wither away like rotting peaches. I wanted to remember Lana in all her lush loveliness.

That left number three.

I took a step forward. She huddled against the wall.

"I ain't gonna turn you over, baby."

A faint, almost disbelieving look of hope crossed Lana's face. "You ... you're not?"

"No. There's too much between us for that. I ain't never forgot you, doll face."

Slowly Lana began to unclench herself from the corner, her

face registering growing confidence as she said, "You'll never … never regret this, Charles." Her voice could've started a fire without matches.

She came towards me, her curves undulating like an ocean in a hurricane.

I waited, enjoying the show.

She reached me, her nose wrinkling slightly as she caught the scent of Old Spice mixed with old zombie, but she recovered quickly. Putting her arms around my neck, Lana pressed herself against me so I could feel every hillock and valley of her voluptuous body.

"I knew you'd change your mind, darling," she murmured, her breath warm in my cold ear.

I smiled, one hand caressing the meat of her firm, rounded ass. "I'd never turn you in, baby," I said, my other hand entwining itself in her luxuriant mane.

"I knew you still loved me." Her voice was triumphant.

"That's right, doll." I pulled her head back so I could see the long, graceful line of her throat. "I want you all to myself." I took a small nibble. "Every single bite."

Well, maybe not every single bite. After all, Larry would be getting up soon and I really couldn't begrudge him.

After all, we did share the same taste in women.

Ringing the Changes

by JEFF SOMERS

Henry used to be a jolly bastard and a lot of fun, but he'd taken the pledge and turned out to be dull as dust when he didn't have a drink in his hand. All he could talk about was his salvation, his sobriety. It was boring stuff. A million weak bastards before him had had the same revelation, and a million more were lining up to dry out after him. Nothing special about it, really, yet people always went on and on about it as if god had reached down and waggled a finger at them and no one else.

At least I was still working, and Henry was pretty good cover. Plus, there wasn't much Henry didn't know about what was happening in outline; his moment of clarity had apparently made old Hankie a good listener, so I felt it was a good idea to stay on his good side, in case I ever needed information. We used to be tight, and he used to be a grand time, so I gave him a little ear-time. I bought him a steady stream of club sodas, which he drank exactly as he'd drunk booze: never putting the glass down, using it to gesture his points, and killing it with a million little sips. If you weren't listening to his endless sermon about giving up The Drink, you'd think his glass was a vodka tonic or a gimlet.

It was slow, and I wasn't making much, so I hurried Henry along. I waved my hand at the bartender and looked at Henry, the dry old bastard.

"Want another?"

"Sure. You shouldn't go so hard, buddy. Believe me, I know."

I nodded, glancing at the bartender. "Another bourbon, kiddo." He looked down at the pile of money on the bar, a crisp fifty right on top, and took my empty glass away. Keeping an eye on him, I inched my hand over and switched the fifty with one of mine from the bottom.

This is what I did. I made people see what I wanted them to see. Even Henry, who didn't notice that my glass was mostly melted ice and watery booze, hardly touched.

The bartender brought my drink and set it in front of me.

"You should charge more for nonalcoholic drinks, buddy," I said, catching his eye. "Discourage the teetotalers, eh?"

He shrugged, plucking the bill off the top, his eyes on me. "Nah. We don't get many in here anyway."

Without glancing at the money, he carried it to the register and rang up my change, bringing back forty-six real dollars and dumping them on the bar. I left them there for a bit, not even looking at them. After a while I'd collect them and put the fifty back on top. For the time being, I studied Henry as if he was the most interesting guy in the world.

"How long'd you do in Rahway?"

Henry nearly lost control of his glass, gesturing. "Three years. Best thing that ever happened to me."

Henry dried out in prison. At first it wasn't voluntary, of course, but then he hooked up with a substance-anonymous crowd and took the pledge. He was going on four years sober now—four sad, desultory, plodding years, but years he was proud of nevertheless.

"Nothing to do but think in prison," he went on. "Not for me, anyway. Some guys found other distractions, but I never had anything except booze."

Henry had no idea how true that was, I suspected, considering his gray, lifeless demeanor post-booze.

"At first all I thought about was booze. You could get some, in prison, but I never could do it. I never had anything to pay with, except my ass, and I wasn't that far gone. So I thought a lot. And I realized that I was in jail because of liquor."

I knew this speech pretty well. Henry got pinched because he'd been loaded. It was pure professionalism that drove the man sober. He never wanted to fuck up again and land back in a place as boring as jail. Henry liked his cable TV.

I stopped listening, letting it wash over me.

Mine wasn't a high-rolling life. I made enough to pay the rent and keep things moving. There were no big scores to be had, I knew this, but there were also few chances at getting killed or arrested if I played it straight. Didn't get fancy. Counterfeit money got traced or sometimes spotted, and a lot of time people remembered me as the guy who spent a lot of fifties. I had to go to different places, work different neighborhoods. If I went to the same place twice, I could get pinched.

My man the bartender wasn't the brightest fellow in the bar, but I didn't think I could pass more than one or two more fifties his way anyway, and Henry was only on chapter one of "How I Won the War," just getting warmed up. So, I gathered up my cash, left a good tip, and stood up. Henry didn't care. He didn't even pause for breath, he just barreled on, giving me the background on his conversion from lush to self-satisfied teetotaler. I knew how it ended —with a lecture from him on why I was a fool to keep drinking.

Which was annoying, since I didn't.

I spoke right over him. "All right, Hankie, I gotta roll."

He trailed off and looked away, insulted. "Yeah, okay."

Walking out of the place, I felt sad. It was a good bar: dark and smoky, wood everywhere, and not filled with complainers. Good jukebox.

***

The Wallace Hotel was hovering between worlds—middle-class decay on the one hand, and people like me on the other. Cheap tourists stayed a few days at a time, or stylish tourists who liked the old-fashioned look of furnishings that hadn't been changed in fifty years.

And then there were people like me. We didn't have jobs or paperwork. We had cash, and an aversion to questions. I've lived there for two years and some weeks, and I've never once spoken with a neighbor. We were all perfect tenants because we didn't shit where we lived. We picked our messages up at the front desk, kept to ourselves, and paid our rent on time. The Wallace, no doubt, wanted more criminals to move in.

I had three rooms, a suite. It was cheap and clean, with a strongbox filled with cash hidden under floorboards beneath the bed; thirty-three thousand dollars, socked away a little at a time. It wasn't a fortune, but it was an insurance policy, a bit of scratch to carry me through a rough patch. I'd earned it all through small, safe grifts. I was careful, slow, and steady.

There was a coffee can in the cupboard with two grand in it. To look at the place, you'd think two grand's about the best I could do. I figured if anyone came snooping, they'd find the coffee can in about five minutes and think that was it.

I worked neighborhoods, using color-copy big bills—twenties and fifties. It wasn't very sophisticated, and it wouldn't pass muster with anyone who knew their currency, but it worked with distracted register jockeys untrained in catching counterfeits. I still got caught from time to time, but I found that I could usually bluff my way out by appearing as surprised as they were. Color-copy counterfeits, even on linen paper, didn't feel like real money, or smell like real money, but since I didn't get greedy, I pulled it off. I'd only print $5100 in fifties, which is thirty-four double-sided copies. That's two bucks each on a self-serve machine unless I could scam free ones. So, for maybe seventy bucks, I had $5100 in worthless money, which I then cut at home, carefully. Then I went shopping.

Most shop owners won't break a fifty for something small, but I wanted as much good money back for each fake as I could manage. I usually began by trying to buy a soda for a dollar, or a buck fifty. If they refused, I explained that I needed change. Sometimes I made forty-eight bucks, sometimes forty. Even at the low end, I made about four grand in a week if I managed to pass all the bills, but finding a hundred places in a week was hard. Each store took time, too. I had to cast the spell and do a little dance, be indecisive, pick up items and put them back, ask a lot of questions, be in a hurry—anything to keep the bastard from looking closely at my money.

The other half of my game had one simple rule: never pay bills with fakes. First off, my fakes were lame, easily spotted ones—I counted on bored, distracted people to accept them without question. Banks, on the other hand, would trace me.

***

The dying afternoon sun sifted through my blinds like dust and warmed the stale air in my suite. I stepped up to the bed, a simple twin with a crappy mattress that came with the place. The only thing I'd done was replace the thin gray mattress with a brand new thin gray mattress. I made money by not spending it, but I drew the line at sleeping with a previous tenant's skin conditions. In fact, news about mattress sales was the only real small talk at The Wallace.

I began emptying my pockets.

Sometimes even I was amazed at how much currency I traded in a day. I tossed bills onto the bed, big sweaty wads of them. I pooled the coins separately, for future sorting. Then, I sat down on the bed and sorted the bills, counting as I went. In bills, I managed three hundred and seventy-three dollars, which wasn't bad for an afternoon that had ended with Henry's lecture of sobriety. I piled the money into neat rubber-banded stacks, pulled out the strong-box, and the place filled with the golden light of upward mobility for a moment, improved the furniture, removed the water stains, and filled the cracks in the walls. I added the cash. A few quick adjustments in the ledger to reflect the new money, and I put everything carefully back where it had been, the strongbox chained to a bolt.

The apartment was transformed back into the last stop on the way down; nothing to see.

I went into the middle room to my bar, which was just a bottle of whiskey and a pitcher of dusty water. I poured two fingers of booze and stood by the grimy windows, yellow light illuminating the dust.

***

I felt tired and heavy. So much effort, just to survive. So I decided on a steak for dinner. I changed into a light suit to go to

Andy's around the corner, where all the waiters had a good-natured competition for my big tips. Down in the lobby, I had messages. One was another grifter seeking a loan, but I had better things to do with my money; it never paid to admit I had enough to lend. The second message was from a police contact, an innocuous note signed "Mr. Blue." I pocketed them both and went to dinner.

My entire life was conducted on borrowed phones. A phone in my room, in my name, was irritating and incriminating, not to mention evidence of income, so I avoided it. At Andy's, I ordered a drink and studied the menu, had the phone brought over, and called the cop. He answered on the fifth ring, sounding breathless.

"Yeah?"

"It's your underground friend."

"Where are you?"

"Andy's on third."

"I'll be there, half an hour. Don't leave."

He hung up. Detective Paul Wilson was middle-aged, unhappy, and not averse to making a few bucks on the side. Nothing major; a little inside information, a little security work for nervous crooks. He never lost sleep over it. I'd had a few minor dealings with him, and we got along well.

I went ahead and ordered dinner. Paul showed up when I was halfway through my steak. He sat down quietly at the table and nodded at me by way of hello.

"Your name came up today," he said. Paul was a heavyset guy, and always sounded out of breath.

"Came up, how?"

"In an investigation. Old business, but nasty. They're gonna come round you up. Ask a lot of questions. I thought I'd just let you know."

"What old business?" I kept eating. There wasn't any point in being dramatic about it.

"All I know is, the vic was named Murray. It was about fifteen years ago, but the case is still open." He shifted in his seat. "That's all I got. Just felt you should know, as an associate."

I chewed, trying to figure out if that meant he thought he could get more money out of me, or if he was dishing some honor-amongst-thieves bullshit, or if it was just simple human respect.

"Okay," I said. "Thanks."

He waited a moment, unsure, and then stood up. "All right. Just thought you should know."

I nodded again and watched him leave. I knew the name Murray, and it was a problem—one I never thought I'd have to deal with. Then again, my associates were criminals. I never knew what they were going to do. Maybe someone gave up my name out of sheer terror, or happened to remember that I'd been in the same room with so-and-so once. I knew I needed to make some calls, but decided to finish my dinner, have some coffee, and relax like a civilized man.

* * *

That was a mistake. The cops, moving with unusual speed, were waiting for me at The Wallace. I didn't get a chance to make my calls. As I walked into my building, I acquired two hefty men in bad suits and gun-crowded shoulders, who pushed me into one of the ancient plush chairs in the lobby and stood over me, making a scene in front of the concierge at the front desk.

"Walter "Poppy" Popvitch?" the one on the left said.

The one on the right didn't wait for an answer. "Where you been, Poppy? We've been waiting for you."

I crossed my legs and regarded them, trying to look calm. "Out to dinner."

"Yeah, so he said, so he said," the one on the left nodded, looking around. "You mind we ask you a few questions?"

I shook my head. "Of course not. Can I ask you what this is about?"

I was selling ignorance, innocence, and confusion but the market was soft. They looked at each other. The one on the right shoved me, lightly. "Come on, let's go back to the station, be friendly."

"Am I under arrest?"

Now, I was selling outrage. This got me nothing but another shove, harder, but still short of a brutality complaint. "Not yet, but it's in your interest to keep us happy, Poppy."

That was annoying; no one called me Poppy. "You don't seem too happy *now*," I pointed out.

The one on the right glanced at his partner, as if saying *See? I told you he wasn't going to be friendly*, and slipped a hand under my armpit, pulling me up, roughly.

"Come on, tough guy," he growled.

They had no warrant, and I wasn't under arrest, but I went quietly, like a good citizen. They only had two questions, but they got good mileage out of them, asking them over and over again.

"Did you know Andrew Murray?"

"No."

"Did you have anything to do with his murder?"

"No."

Between repeating their two questions, they jabbered on with a few scary details and hints that they had something on me. They didn't, though. If they had, I would have been under arrest. So, after a few hours, they let me go to think about it and put a tail on me. But I didn't care. I had nothing to hide; not much, anyway. I went back to Andy's, borrowed the phone at the bar, and made my few calls. After half a beer and a lot of dial tones, I tracked down Henry and told him I'd buy him dinner if he'd come down and let me pick his brain. Henry never turned down a free meal, and he knew everything about everyone.

When Henry showed up ten minutes later, I wanted to grill him immediately about Murray, but first, there were pleasantries. I'd offended Henry at our last meeting, and he walked in the place with the wounded air of a true martyr—a sober martyr at that, the worst kind. But I couldn't really blame him; since he'd lost the courage booze had given him, Henry made a good part of his living dealing and acquiring information, so it made sense that he'd want to keep things chatty, and I'd walked out on him mid-sentence. It was damned annoying, though, when I needed information and wanted to shake the bastard until his valuable head popped off.

I bought Henry a soda and let him harangue me about the lush Scotch on the rocks I was nursing. I endured him waving the glass under my nose, thick finger outstretched, as he delivered a sermon about the Rules of Polite Society and how you treated people the way you wanted to be treated yourself. Finally, he sighed piteously and bought me a drink, and I jumped in to bring up business before he could gather his energies for the standard higher-power sermon Henry liked to end all his tirades with these days.

"I've been hearing a lot about an old piece of business, Hankie, but I can't seem to place the details."

"What business would that be?" he asked, sagging slightly until he seemed to be hanging off the bar.

"Somebody named Murray, gone to lavender a few years ago."

He closed his eyes and settled himself on the stool. Watching Henry think was more interesting than expected. He went into a trance and fidgeted, twitching and raising his eyebrows, scanning back through his photographic memory.

"Okay," he said, his eyes popping open. "I think I've heard about this."

"Good. How far back did you have to go?"

"Oh—about ten."

I nodded. A hundred bucks was cheap. And, it meant that he didn't see much value in the information, so was offering it at a discount. "Good number."

He closed his eyes again. "Andrew Murray, pickpocket. Worked the East Side, mostly. Subsistence kind of career, only big scores were accidental, whatever he happened to pinch. Not real smooth, either. Got caught several times, never arrested, beaten up a few times. Found dead in a public lavatory in Grand Central Station seven years ago, apparently beaten to death with a blunt instrument. Police assumed it was a pocketing gone wrong and didn't wind themselves looking into it. Case remains open.

"Word around town is that it was a fellow grifter did it. No names, just rumors. Doubt that some civilian could have whacked him, posed him in the can, and not leave a trace—must have been someone with skills. He had a lot of enemies, could have been anyone that he owed money to, which were plenty. He drank and gambled and liked to have whores on hand. He liked to live a flashy life on a very small income, and got in deep with shylocks, not to mention anyone dumb enough to give him a friendly loan. Drank like a fish and it sank him in the end. Your basic black hole. We've all known this guy, and kept our distance. I used to be this guy."

He looked at me meaningfully, trying to communicate, no doubt, that he thought there was a little bit of black hole in *me*. I rattled the ice in my drink as a talisman and nodded, amazed—I wondered briefly what Henry would have been capable of if he hadn't soaked his brain in liquor for thirty years. But I was satisfied. Nothing unexpected.

"As you know," Henry went on after a moment, "your name comes into it."

I froze, careful not to reveal the shock. I took a sip from my drink, nodding.

"Let's talk about that."

Without opening his eyes, he raised both eyebrows. "Indeed. Let's. There's no direct connection, I don't think. It's a case of degrees of separation. The last person the police believe saw Murray was Miles Tucker. Tucker couldn't be tracked down for years; he'd left the city, and efforts to locate him and his various names and pseudonyms—as lackluster as they were—were fruitless until a week ago when Tuck reappeared at some old haunts, cheerful and buying drinks. Scooped up by some bored crushers, he provided your name as a get-out-of-jail-free card."

"Oh shit," I exhaled, draining my glass. I remembered Tuck, vaguely. Hadn't known him well and couldn't remember if he'd been there that night, but it was possible. It was feasible. I spent my whole life spinning the feasible into reality. I knew how it worked.

"Dismayed, Walt? That's either a fabrication or an inconvenience to you. Either way, the police will no doubt haunt you for a bit."

I nodded, signaling the bartender for another round. The fucking cops hadn't mentioned this guy's alibi to me, but that just meant Tuck wasn't very reliable and the cops were shaking the tree, seeing what fell out.

I dug out two more C-notes and slid them over to Henry. He looked at me.

"Tuck's real name," I said, accepting a fresh drink from the bartender gratefully. "And where he might be found."

Henry made the bills disappear. "Indeed," he said, managing to sound aggrieved about earning money.

***

After leaving Henry, I let the cops watch me go home. I fixed myself a cup of coffee and sat at the kitchen table for an hour, drinking and thinking. No one gave a shit about this clown Murray. The cops were looking for a quick and easy clearance. They wanted names they could take to court, and I doubted they cared much about the truth. And there I was, plain as day, for the cops to turn over and see what crawled out. I intended to remove myself from the equation.

My coffee finished, I changed into an old suit, opened up the bathroom window, and climbed out. From there, I was able to climb up onto the roof of the building next door. It was dangerous, but I'd done it before. I ran across my building and jumped over to another roof. Three more jumps, and I was able to climb down a series of fire escapes and emerge on the street several blocks away. I hailed a cab, gave the driver an address a few blocks away from the one Henry had given me. Then, I spent some time looking out the back window for pursuit. I didn't see any, so I relaxed, watching the city go by.

The taxi let me off in a dingy, run-down neighborhood—I knew this one; knew where it was safe to spend my money and where I'd get broken hands for my trouble. I walked briskly to the address Tuck was using, bristling with anger. I remembered this fuck. We had nothing between us, I thought, but here he was, trying to jam me up. It pissed me off.

His brownstone, weathered and chipped, was in the middle of the block. The streetlight was broken, leaving the house in a shadow. This wasn't the sort of work I was used to doing, but I did what I had to do.

I walked up and rang the bell. The rest happened quickly.

The door opened, and an unfamiliar shape filled the space. I didn't pause to be sure, or to be clean. My knife came out, and I leaned in. I pushed it forward and up, pulled it out, then back again, punching him. He leaned backward, trying to climb up off my blade, but he leaned too far, and he toppled over. I stepped in and shut the door behind me. I looked down at Tucker. I was glad he wasn't some poor ass who got in the way, but regardless, this is how it had to be done—fast and thoughtless.

***

Sometimes, I cut a corner each off of four twenty-dollar bills and pasted the corners onto a one-dollar bill. It's surprising how often this works when a cashier is busy or stressed. It's a quick, dirty, and dangerous way to make a fast $100 or so; making people see something that isn't there.

This is what I did. I moved quickly through the house, and when I was sure there was no one else, I left the knife in the sink and climbed out the bathroom window. I got home in an hour, walking the whole way. I didn't see any blood on me, but I wouldn't be sure until I got home. I climbed back in the way I'd gone out, inspected myself, and stripped, tossing everything into the garbage.

After a hot, hot shower, I stepped into a robe and felt good. I peeked out a window and checked out the cops, reliable as the sun. I made myself a coffee, and the cops saw what I wanted them to see. It's what I do.

The Kilt

by ROMAN BOJANSKI

Now that I'm almost out of my mess, I started thinking that when you step inside one of those payday loan places—where they charge fraudulent rates of interest for loans based on your pay stub—they should have a steamy pile of shit that you walk in when entering. Because if you don't know that you're walking into a heaping pile when you get in there, you will. I needed the money, and I wasn't making enough. So I got my loans in complete denial that at best I was on the road to bankruptcy. After those tallies mounted and I couldn't pay them back, I found a loan shark. Never caring if loan sharks really existed, or thinking I'd ever need one, or know how to get one when I did, I was a bit dazed going through the whole process. To complete the trifecta, I started betting to pay the payday loans and the loan shark back. The only thing I succeeded at was selling everything I owned, losing the life I had, and leveling my markers off at $28,000 in the hole. My life is shit, I don't own anything anymore. I'm 35 and I eat Ramen noodles most every meal. I rent a walk-in closet from an ex-con. All my money feeds the sharks.

But finally, after weeks of not believing it, I am on my way to Mackey the bookie's bar, to collect $30,000 because I bet the long odds on the Detroit Pistons winning the championship. If only this cop would let me go.

He hasn't approached the car yet and I've been sitting here five minutes with my pad of paper out watching the flicker of his blue and red flashers. I've got notes written, thinking if I played like I can't talk, I'd get out of getting the car towed and could make it to Mackey and close my account, and move on. Finally the cop climbs from his car and walks toward me.

I roll down the window and hand him my first note before he can say anything: *Sorry Officer, I can't talk—chronic laryngitis for three days now. I'm on my way to pick up my brother, it's an emergency.*

The office looks at the note, and asks, "Driver's license please."

I pull it out of my wallet, and hand it to him with the second note: *This is my brother's car. I live with him while I'm sick. He needs me to pick him up because he has an important job interview.*

If I don't pick up that $30,000 by 4:30, then Mackey's bar opens and I'm not allowed to pick it up until tomorrow. At midnight tonight my loans flip and I'm $32,000 in the hole. After midnight I'm still fucked. If I make it by 4:30, I'm golden.

"Do you realize you're burning oil and dripping fluids as you drive down the road?"

The car is my brother's. After I had to turn in the title on mine, my brother had this piece-of-shit Buick that his kids ran into the ground. He was going to get rid of it, but I said I needed it. And I said that I needed him to keep the title in his name, and that I needed to drive it without insurance. He wouldn't normally let me, but fucking the hot chick at the end of the block wasn't enough to get his wife to leave him, so he's trying to pull some other shit to piss her off.

I scribble this note as the cop watches. *It's just an emergency car that I've never driven before. He's stranded out on Route 88 and can't get a cab. He has an interview. I thought I'd help him.*

When loan sharks and bookies are holding you by the balls, you have no room to lie. When you have moved into some weirdo-loser's apartment because he charges you cheap rent to sleep in a walk-in closet, you don't even speak a word because acknowledging the freak's presence and establishing a relationship with him only drives home the fact that you're a fucking loser, too. So I haven't had a chance to lie in years, since I started owing people so much money. This laryngitis thing and the notes feels good—like a release.

It's relatively hot outside and the car has no AC so I'm sweating all over myself and the pad of paper.

"Wait here," the cop says and walks back to his car.

It's 2:45. Mackey's bar is out on Route 88, one of the stretches of road that's in the middle of the suburbs but not surrounded by suburbs. It's nestled among the shipping canal and junkyards which all sit in a stretch of green forest for a mile before you see your first strip mall. After that for miles and miles around its split levels and strip malls, but over there by the junkyards it feels secluded, remote. And in the thicket is Mackey's bar—The Kilt. I've never met Mackey but they say he's a big dude, former college football player, and he always wears a kilt. It's a twenty- or thirty-minute drive from here.

At 3:03 the cop finally comes back to the car. Eighteen fucking minutes and I am going crazy and my arms are dripping sweat and my forehead has beads of sweat, and I'm sure my back is one big, dark wet spot.

I have a one-word note written to him when he gets back to the car:

Please.

"How do you know your brother needs help?"

I scribble as fast as I can: *He called me.*

"How did you talk to him?"

Scribbling again: *One tap 'no.' Two taps 'yes.'* And I motion like I'm holding a phone in my hand and show my index finger tapping.

"Can I call your brother and confirm your story?"

Please. Please. Please. Motherfucking please.

I write: *I don't have a cell phone.* Then I think the cop probably does. So I hesitate to give him that note. I flip to a new page. *His cell phone is dead. He was calling me from a pay phone.*

Can you believe the patience on this guy? To sit there while I scribble notes? Really fucking amazing.

"Where do you live?" I write down my address. "Why doesn't your license match?" He's trying to get rapid fire and break me out of my routine and see what he can mess up; maybe even to see if I'll speak. I scribble an answer as fast as I can. "Where is your brother at that he needs a ride?"

I write, *The Kilt.*

"He's going to a job interview and he's leaving from *The Kilt?*"

I write, *It's desperate.*

"You don't have to tell me that." Then he looks up to the sky, and says, "Fuck." He looks back down at me and says, "Unbelievable," and takes my license off his clipboard.

As fast and as big as I can, I write, *Thank You.*

I start the car while the cop returns to his squad. When I look in my mirror to see what he's doing, I can't see anything because of the heavy purple smoke pouring out from my exhaust as I rev the engine. As the smoke blows away and I can barely make out what's behind me, I'm off. I look at the clock for the millionth time that minute amazed that it's still 3:14.

Did I say, finally I'm a winner? So close.

I do my best to drive towards Route 88 and look like I don't know my car is a heaping pile of shit. Anytime I have to drive it—which is rarely since I started taking the bus to work—I just look ahead and avoid glancing laterally at the people whipping by scowling at being smoked out. Horns honk and people yell at me and I hear "fuckhead" and "shitface" and "loser" all the time. When I choose to acknowledge hearing them I usually raise my eyebrows as if to say, 'Nothing worse than what I call myself.'

Twenty-five miles an hour and hitting every stop light (because I can't join the flow of traffic) is the only way I'll make it. Going that slow only makes it worse for the car because the wind can't find its way to the engine to cool anything down. But I have to go slow, which makes the car hot, and that means I drive with the heat full blast to keep the engine cool and running.

As I get within fifteen minutes of the place, the oil light starts to flicker on and off.

"Fuck you," I tell it.

The fast flicker is followed by another blinking of the temperature gauge.

"Fuck off," I say, quietly, "Not now."

It's amazing the steering wheel can shake any more than it does, since the bearings in the wheels are shot and I'm missing at least one lug nut on each tire. But it can, and now it starts to shake and shimmy.

"Not now motherfucker," I say, calmly, as if I were staring down a big rhinoceros and thinking if I only play it cool, trouble will go away. But I've got sweat pouring out of my body because it's 85 degrees out and probably 110 in the car.

"No," I say quick and firm.

The shimmy does get harder.

"NO." More insistent.

"NOOOOO." A long firm one.

The shakes are violent now. The steering wheel shouldn't be able to move so much, so hard, and so fast.

It feels like I'm inside the fucking spin cycle of an unbalanced washing machine.

"Fuck you, you motherfucker!"

Instead of hitting the breaks because this entire machine feels like it's going to snap; I gun it thinking whatever kinks are in the system, maybe I can just blow through them. I slam the gas to the floor. And the only thing I hear is a PING above the rumble. Then its the fast and furious sound of heavy machinery coming to a grinding halt as all the oil in the engine must have burned up and the pistons and the valves and any other moving part in the thing reached it's breaking point, got so hot it burned all the oil lubricating the movement between parts so they just get hotter and hotter until the pistons and the cylinders begin to melt, which means the friction is so high they practically stick together. That's when everything just seizes.

Poof. And the final smoke signal takes flight from the exhaust in a light, effervescent cloud of gray. That one small burden is laid down, which only means I'm completely fucked at 3:37 in the afternoon.

I pop the hood, and in the slight two-inch opening before the latch can be undone black smoke releases, and lilts away. I hit the hazards, which fortunately still work. In desperation I try to restart the engine. No way. Not a movement, not a click.

As the smoke clears I put the car in neutral, get out, and push-steer it into the gas station a half block away.

Running into the phone booth, I call the nearest cab company. Given that I'm in the suburbs, cabs take forever to get here.

160

"It'll be thirty minutes."

"Are you sure?"

"At least."

Not sure if I can make it by then, I say, "Okay, send him."

In the meantime, I ask people while they're pumping gas if they could possibly give me a ride. 3:46 and I know what it must feel like to be a bum shaking the cup on the street. People say 'No,' before you can ask them. Anyone with a decent car that could maybe give money? They don't even look.

"No," I hear, and "Sorry," and "Can't do it." And I try to reason that it's only fifteen minutes away, and probably in the direction they're already heading in. Nothing works.

The attendant comes out of the office, "What are you going to do with your car?"

"Worry about it in an hour."

"No you don't. I'll call the cops."

"They'll be happy the thing's off the road." Then I realize that if the same cop shows and I'm screaming and yelling, I'm totally fucked. So I tell the guy, "I just called a cab and the junk yard, they'll be here shortly."

That's it! The junkyard is across the street from The Kilt. If they can get over here, hitch the car up and bring it back, I can get let out across the street, walk in, take my cash, and maybe even get fifty bucks for the car.

Running to the phone booth, I call the salvage yard on 88 and ask how long it will take to pick up my junker.

"Our driver gets off at 4:00," the guy says, "I don't think he'll want to get it until the morning."

"Is he still there?" I ask.

"Yeah, just walked in."

"Can I talk to him and ask?"

"Sure," the guy says, seemingly holds the phone out on the other end and says, "Timo, guy wants his car picked up today. Wanna talk to him?"

There's a rustle as the phone is being handed over. The phone is dropped. It's picked back up and a guy asks, "Lo?" in a deep Mexican accident.

"Hi Timo, this is Rob," I say, "My car broke down and I want it picked up. But I need to get to The Kilt before 4:30 or I'm fucked."

Timo starts laughing on the other end of the phone.

I ignore him and continue, "I will tip you tremendously if you came to get me now."

Timo shouts to everyone else in the room, "His car broke and he's got to get over to The Kilt by 4:30." There's a chorus of laughter going off in the background.

"Timo, this isn't funny," I plea, "I can't miss this appointment."

Timo's chuckling on the other end, and gets serious for a second before saying, "No bro," with a breathy laugh, "I got to pick my kids up from daycare and can't spare the half hour," He's laughing some more, "Sorry bro."

"Timo," I say, "C'mon ..."

"Sorry bro, I truly am," he huffs some laughter out and hangs up.

3:53. Fucked. So fucked. I swear I will do anything to get to the bar by 4:30. I'm thinking about clocking someone and stealing their car, or just car jacking it while they're inside. That'll just lead to another whole set of problems. Because when I talked to Mackey's man, he asked if I was going to place another bet with my winnings.

"No way, man, I'm out," I had said.

He asked, "You're not doing business with Mackey anymore?"

"I'd rather go on food stamps and live in public housing. My life is shit and I'm cashing out and staying out."

"Okay, then you have to pick up your final winnings from Mackey himself.' He told me all about the pick-up procedure and protocol. Then, before he got off the phone, he'd said, 'Don't bring any trouble to The Kilt, or you're fucked, literally."

"What?"

"Just don't."

Right now, I'm fucked literally. That's when I spot a guy rolling in driving a white Ford F-150 with rusted out fenders and balding tires. Screw asking people with nice cars who should be the happy, helpful members of society. Here's a guy around my age who looks like he's had the same amount of troubles I have, so I'm going over to him.

I give him a nod well before I'm within speaking distance to let him know I'm going to talk to him, and I'm harmless. When I get over there he's pumping his gas and I say, "Hey man, I'm in a desperate situation."

He looks at me like he's listening.

"I need to get to The Kilt by 4:30 and my car broke down."

He seems to be holding back laughter. But I am on a fucking mission so I blow by his reaction in favor of telling my sob story.

"Sure I'll take you."

"Great!" I say, "Thanks, dude, my name's Rob, and you are like a fucking miracle."

"No problem," he says smirking. "Lemme go pay and we'll hit it."

I get into the passenger side, and I know we're going to make it. No problems. We're fifteen or twenty minutes away, tops. I keep looking to see if the guy is going to stall and have some problem inside with the cashier. But nope, he's paid up and walking out, and the truck starts fine, and he puts it into gear.

"Truck runs smooth," I say.

"This truck is amazing."

After all that excitement I just sit back and relax. But the guy pipes in and asks:

"How'd you get mixed up with The Kilt?"

"All the wrong ways, all the wrong reasons."

"You know somebody who's, um," he clears his throat, "dealt with Mackey before?"

"Nope, it's kind of a fluke how I got involved, and more of a surprise that I'm getting out."

The drive goes smoothly. The Kilt is like three blocks away now and my watch reads 4:11.

"Lemme just tell you, Mackey is the low man on the gambling ring totem pole. Sure, he has his own book, but he's not like the rest of the guys who run numbers."

"I don't get it."

"I personally never dealt with him, but," he pauses, "You probably won't again either."

Damn right to that. I'm practically jumping out of the seat when we slide into the gravel parking lot. That junkyard is there, and Timo's probably already gone. I'll have them pick up my car tomorrow. I'm going to pick up the money and walk all the way to the loan shark if I have to, and get there in plenty of time, and tomorrow I'm calling in sick to work, again, and I'm just going to go outside and look at the sunshine and feel the warmth and think of them as something other than light and heat. They're going to be warm and healthy, and I'm going to be happy to be outside.

"Hey, if you want to wait inside while I do the pick up, I'll be able to pay you $100 dollars. I'm that grateful."

"I can't go in there with you," He says, "Otherwise you'd be fucked."

I can't stop and pause and think that one over, all I can do is say, "Thanks a lot," and jump out and hustle in. Heading into the dark bar with the bartender cleaning the glasses is almost like a movie, except the guy behind the bar is prettier than the old timer I would expect to see. He wears a fashionable western-like shirt with pearl buttons and his hair is styled perfectly. New-age bookie.

"Mackey's in back," He says, "Go through that door that says, *Do Not Enter*."

I walk quickly back there; I open the door. Inside the room is brightly lit. It seems to be a private bar room, because Mackey—I know it's him because he's sitting there with a kilt on, is sitting on a bar stool at the bar with a highball glass filled with ice and some brown liquor. Next to him is a guy not much taller than me, skinny, wearing a black sweater, black slacks, black shoes—whole black deal. He's got a crew cut and a beard of the same length and he looks gaunt.

"Made it," I say.

"Almost there," Mackey says, "Now come over here."

This is it. I'm out of here, a winner for the first time in years. Tomorrow is a new day. Today is forgotten. I'm willing to bet right now that I'll be so happy tomorrow that I'll never think about this day again. Maybe the troubles before this I'll remember as a cautionary tale, but today I can forget about because the story will be about the loss and the final win, and that's all already taken place.

"It's 4:16," Mackey says.

I'm standing about five feet from him.

"Come, stand right here," he says and points to the spot right next to him.

I move a couple of feet closer but not right next to him. He's wearing a gray polo shirt, short sleeves, with a blue, green, and gray kilt. Gray socks, and heavy black shoes, with those oil-proof soles that gas station workers wear. His arm closest to me has a barbed-wire wraparound tattoo. He's got strawberry blond hair and his face is large, with drooping cheeks that hang from his face almost lower than his protruding chin. Offensive lineman probably. He's big and hairy but not obese.

The gaunt motherfucker takes a step closer too. He pulls two four inch stacks of money out of his pockets, and says:

"Thirty," in a very deep voice, his Adam's apple bobbing.

He pulls back his sweater sleeve and looks at his watch.

"Four-seventeen." Then he lifts something off the stool next to Mackey, twists it, and I recognize the spin of a timer. He sets it down on the bar in front of Mackey, closer to me than the money, and says, "Thirteen minutes."

I'm dazed. I don't say anything. It doesn't feel like I'm expected to.

The bartender opens the door, "It's all clear," popping his head in, "No trouble."

Then the gaunt guy takes two more things out. First, he draws a snub nose thirty-eight revolver and makes sure I see him holding it in his hand. And lastly, he lifts something off the stool that was next to the timer. The timer is humming as it counts down. The other thing is a bottle. He takes that bottle and sets it practically right in front of me. Jergens lotion.

"Twelve minutes, thirty seconds," the gaunt guy says and walks over to guard the door of the room, gun still in his hand.

Mackey looks at me and says, "Like I said, you're almost there."

I'm choking on the lack of words in my throat. He stares at me for a second to make sure I get it. Then in case I'm as stupid as I look, he adds:

"To get this," he says pointing to the stacks of money, "you might need to use this," and motions to the lotion. Then he leans back in the bar stool. And with his lips partially open he looks at me and peels back his kilt.

I feel a squirrelly smile on my face as I look at him, because, even if I didn't want to believe it myself, I knew today would have a happy ending.

Faggy on the Streets

by JEFFREY DINSMORE

He stands triumphant, or, as the Chinese say, triumphalist. A man of the streets. A player. Nobody's fool, this one. He'll take you downtown on the Brown line and when he do, he won't buy you no breakfast or cook you no Steak-umms, no way, baby. He'll take you down to where you need to go and he'll say to you, "Look, there, that's where you belong, you maggot." Maybe he'll have you by the collar, maybe he won't need to have his hands anywhere near you, depending on what kind of mood he's in and how much chicken shit you got in ya'.

That's the man, right there. That's how he do, and when he do, you do, too.

They call him Faggy. John Faggy. And he is one badasssss cracker.

***

"Gather round, ladies," the chief barked. "We've got some serious shit going down today and we're gonna need everyone out on the beat."

The detectives of Shaker City's 12th precinct made their way back to the conference room. Notably absent was Guitarzan, who had been gunned down by the Palermo cartel the week before. Faggy felt no sympathy for Guitarzan or his family. Guitarzan was the kind of cop who let things get sloppy, one of those "cop by day, wrestler by night" types. At Guitarzan's funeral, Faggy had ruffled a few feathers by spitting on his grave. "I hope they got donuts in Hell," Faggy had said.

"Where's Punkin?" the chief asked, when the detectives were assembled.

"He's on the phone with his bookie, chief."

"Punkin!" the chief shouted. "Make your bets on your own dime. We got drugs to bust."

Punkin begrudgingly joined the other detectives in the meeting room.

"What the fuck, Punkin?" the hard-talking chief asked.

"What the fuck, chief?" Punkin shot back.

"All right, settle down," the chief began. "As I said before, there's some serious shit going down today. Serious shit. Word on the street is that the Palermos are making a big move, and we're running interference. Kilganey and Pawks, I need you on lookout by the docks. You see anything out of the ordinary, I want you on the squawk box."

Kilganey and Pawks gave each other the serious high-five.

"Molero, I want you to work the crack houses on the Lower East Side. See what you can find out about the delivery—where it came from, who's buying, and who they work for."

"For whom they work, chief," corrected Molero.

"Go fuck yourself, Molero. And if I catch you hitting the pipe again, you're gonna be in some serious shit."

Molero nodded.

"Now, Faggy ..." the captain began.

All eyes turned toward the star of the team. Faggy sat on the desk at the front of the room, one leg up, picking his teeth with a fork. Dark glasses shaded his eyes from the harsh light of reality. The constant pained expression on his face pointed to a darker sort of pain inside, the kind of pain that can only be cured by ridding the world of evil, one motherfucker at a time.

Faggy swung his leg off the desk and pushed himself to his feet. When standing erect, his six foot three-inch frame and double-barrel pecs made for an imposing presence. Behind the glasses, his eyes betrayed no emotion.

"Faggy, why don't you just do what you do?" the chief asked.

Faggy nodded.

"Gonna need some backup," he said.

"Backup, sure. Why don't you take the new kid, Squeamish?"

At the mention of his name, Squeamish looked up. Finally, some fucking action. Since he joined the force a few weeks ago, he'd been pushing papers around his desk, waiting patiently for one of the hot shots to ask him out on the beat. John Faggy was the hottest cop of them all, 6 feet and 3 inches of pure action. This was gonna be good.

Faggy stared a hole through the back of the chief's head. When everyone was good and uncomfortable, he slowly nodded.

"Class dismissed," Faggy growled.

***

Faggy drove. Faggy always drives. He's the kind of rubber-burning macho hot-rod rider who can get your ass out of some serious situations. Car chases? Oh man, you better believe it. John

Faggy will run you down two times before you even get your key in the ignition.

"So, your name's Faggy, huh?" asked Squeamish. "You get a lot of shit for that?"

Faggy suddenly slammed on the brakes and fishtailed the car into an empty spot on the crowded city streets, and it was fucking beautiful. The force of the sudden stop jerked Squeamish forward into his seatbelt. Faggy turned the engine off and leaned over to stare directly into Squeamish's face.

"Listen, motherfucker," he said, forcefully, "I'm not here to be your fucking buddy. I don't wanna hear about your frigid wife or your rotten kids or the asshole at the dry cleaner's who left a taco stain on your uniform. I approved of you as my backup 'cause I can't stand any of the rest of those pricks. I need you to keep your fucking mouth shut and your eyes open for people who are going to shoot me. Capisce?"

Squeamish nodded.

Faggy chuckled.

"I like you, kid. Now let's hit the streets."

First stop was Silent Slim's Stereo Shack. Slim's the kinda guy who knows stuff. Trouble with Slim is you gotta give to get. Today, Faggy served up a juicy little tidbit about a bust that was going down next week in Pinkwater. In exchange, Slim let slip that people in the know were referring to the Palermo deal as Operation Big Turkey.

"Faggy, why did you tell that guy about the bust in Pinkwater?" Squeamish asked when they were back out on the street. "If that information falls into the wrong hands, people could get killed."

"As the Chinese say, 'All human life is disposable,'" Faggy answered. "Go wait in the car, Squeamish. I've gotta fuck a prostitute."

Not just for pleasure, this one. John Faggy doesn't do anything just for pleasure. The prostitute in question was Lil Diamond, sister of Big Diamond, the lower East Side's king of discount crack. Faggy knew that when Lil was satisfied sexually, she was like an open book, and Faggy never left a woman wanting. He humped her so hard and good that she was still screaming his name for the next few days. In between screams, he managed to get some hot info on Operation Big Turkey.

"John Faggy! My brother told me that oh, Faggy! Operation Big Turkey was put together by some Faggy! new guys, group that calls themselves the shit, Faggy! Enforcers John Faggy!"

Faggy gave the bitch a smack on the ass and high-tailed it back to the car, where Squeamish was busy twiddling his thumbs with his dick.

"Anything?" Squeamish asked.

"Listen, kid, I'm gonna drop kick you through that window if you don't shut the fuck up. We're going back to the office."

Back at HQ, Faggy had Elaine run a check on Enforcers. Turns out, the name had been mentioned in connection with Guitarzan's death the week before.

"We're holding a suspect out on Cable Island. Klaus Werner. You should be able to get some information out of him."

"Thanks, Elaine," said Faggy. "You're the only twat in this office who knows what she's doing."

***

Faggy and Squeamish sat at a visitors' desk, waiting for Klaus Werner to arrive. They sat silent, some might even say brooding. Faggy didn't like coming to jail. Too many bad memories. He'd given half the fuckers in this place their admission papers. On Cable

Island, all eyes were on Faggy. All it took was one jive turkey with a shiv to put an end to what had been a brilliant career in law enforcement.

The guard led Werner to the desk in handcuffs. What a fucking piece of Eurotrash this guy was. 'Welcome to my discotheque, you scumbag,' Faggy thought.

"Hello, Vaggy," Werner said, in stiffly accented English.

Faggy slammed his hands down on the desk.

"All right, you stinking piece of garbage, I don't like you and you don't like me, but if you don't tell me everything you know about the Enforcers right now, I'm gonna introduce you to the sweatiest, meanest bulldog in this place and laugh as he fucks you in half."

Werner smiled slightly. He had his own troubles to deal with in prison, but at least he was safely locked away from Detective John Faggy.

"Don't know too much," Werner replied, "Zay are new players. Zay do all zere business tru a middle man, Colombo Spitz. Last I knew, he vas staying at ze Villish Inn on Decatur."

Faggy stood and spit a fierce loogie into Werner's face.

"Fuck you," Faggy said. Then, turning to Squeamish, he screamed, "Get the fuck up, Squeamish! Let's roll!"

Squeamish sighed and pushed his chair back from the table.

"You know, you could be nicer to me," Squeamish said, as they hotfooted it out of the prison.

Faggy chuckled and shook his head.

"You're all right, kid."

***

The Village Inn is located five miles outside of the city near the

Epson Expressway. A real shithole, this place, one of the many unmemorable halfway homes dotting the perimeter of the city, filled with perverts and fuckups with something to hide. Faggy gritted his teeth as he pulled into the parking lot. Someone was about to get real bloody.

Faggy instructed Squeamish to hang out in the parking lot and keep his eyes pealed for suspicious characters. Meanwhile, the renegade detective headed into the hotel office to track down Colombo Spitz.

Faggy flung the door open forcefully.

"Hey, dickhead," he shouted to the mealy-looking fucker behind the desk, "Which room is Spitz staying in?"

"Now listen here," said the man behind the desk, clearly agitated, "No one talks to me like that in my hotel."

That was all the push Faggy needed. He jumped across the counter and brought his full weight down on top of the owner. The owner crumpled to the ground and starting sobbing like the little girl he was.

"Colombo Spitz, you son of a bitch!" Faggy shouted, holding his pistol to the owner's temple.

"214! 214!" the owner screamed back.

Faggy stood up and lifted the owner to his feet.

"Now, that wasn't so hard, was it?" he asked.

The owner slumped back into his chair, bruised and frightened.

As Faggy headed toward the door, the owner shouted after him.

"Who are you?"

Faggy turned around and lowered his shades down the bridge of his nose.

"They call me ... Faggy."

The owner gave him a quizzical look.

"Well, everyone's welcome here," he said.

Out in the parking lot, Faggy pointed at Squeamish and mouthed the words, "Let's roll." Squeamish removed his gun from the holster and followed his partner up the stairs to Room 214.

Faggy pushed his weight against the doorframe and burst into the room. Empty. In the ashtray, a still smoldering cigarette pointed to a recent escape.

"Goddammit!" Faggy screamed.

Squeamish turned around to see a deeply tanned man running across the parking lot.

"Faggy!" Squeamish yelled. "Down there!"

Faggy shoved Squeamish out of the way as he ran out onto the balcony. Squinting, he fired two shots from his pistol into the thigh of the running man. Was it mentioned that Faggy was a crack shot? Did it need to be? This motherfucker could shoot a toothpick out of your peehole from fifty yards away and leave your mushroom head smooth as silk.

Squeamish and Faggy ran down the stairs to the parking lot, where the tanned man lay bleeding and gasping for breath. Faggy leaned down next to him.

"When and where is it going down, Spitz?" Faggy asked.

"4:00," Spitz spat. "Pier 32."

"And who are the Enforcers?"

"They are ... they're led by ..." Spitz drooled, beginning to lose consciousness.

Faggy reared back and gave Spitz a hard punch in the chops.

"Spit it out, Spitz!" he screamed.

" ... "

"Aahhhhh! Aahhhhh!" Faggy screamed in Spitz's face.

With the last bit of strength in his body, Spitz managed to push out one final word.

"Punkin."

"Goddammit!" Faggy yelled, then grabbed Squeamish by the lapels and threw him full force against the side of the squad car.

"Jesus fucking Christ, Faggy!" Squeamish said, picking himself up off the ground. "Get a hold of yourself!"

Faggy threw his head back and let out a deep belly laugh.

"Oh, shit, kid, you're a pisser," he laughed.

***

4:00. Pier 32. One man stands alone. Only this time, he's got backup. And this ain't no namby-pamby slackjaw looking to fill his quota on parking tickets; no sir. This one's the real fucking deal. Officer Ray Squeamish. He's been around the block a few times. He's seen shit that would make you wish you'd never been born. He wasn't always like this, hell no. Couple of hours ago he was filling in boxes on a Scantron sheet, waiting to be chosen like a fat girl at the debutante's ball. No longer. Faggy made him hard.

Faggy scanned the pier for signs of his fellow officers. Nothing. Just the wind whistling through his hair and the smell of cod wafting off the fishing boats. But Faggy detected something else in the air. He breathed in deeply. That was it. The smell of crime, with a hint of rotten pig.

Faggy pointed at a catamaran docked just off the Pier. Squeamish nodded. No words necessary between these two. They'd paid their dues together and now they were going to reap their rewards ... in blood.

The two officers crouched low and made their way onto the ship. The deck buckled and swayed in the roiling ocean. In the distance, storm clouds farted across a tortured sky. Staying low to the ground, they crawled over to the cabin. They could detect two men inside, speaking in hushed tones. Faggy pulled a shot glass from his pocket and pressed it against the side of the cabin.

"Joo got the stuff?" asked one man, in a thick Spanish accent.

"Yeah, I got it," replied the other. Faggy cringed. It was unmistakably the voice of Pete Punkin, officer of the law.

Suddenly, the cabin door burst open, and in rushed Detective Molero.

"Freeze, motherfuckers!" Molero shouted. "Hand over the powder!"

Faggy and Squeamish couldn't sit back and watch the action unfurl any longer, not these two. These two were pumped and ready to explode. With a mighty war cry, they crashed through the window of the cabin and dropped to the ground, pointing their pistols at Punkin.

"I always knew you were an asshole, Punkin," Faggy said. "But I never took you for crooked."

"No, it's not like that, Faggy," Punkin pleaded. "It's a double sting! Everyone knows Molero's a crackhead! He just wants the drugs!"

"Did joo just call that guy faggy?" the Spanish-speaking man whispered to Punkin.

Faggy and Squeamish turned their guns on Molero.

"Is that true, Molero? Got a monkey on your back, needs a little taste?"

"No, Faggy!" Molero shouted. "This bastard is up to his ears in gambling debts! He's looking for the big payoff!"

"Fuck!" Faggy screamed.

He turned to Squeamish.

"What the fuck do we do, Squeamish?" he asked.

Were Squeamish a contemplative man, he might have recognized this moment as a sign of utmost respect. John Faggy didn't take advice from anyone, yet here he was, asking for help. If Squeamish were a thinking man, he might have seen this as a passing of the torch.

But Ray Squeamish was neither of those things. Ray Squeamish was a soldier. A soldier of the law.

"Kill them all!" Squeamish screamed, firing three shots into Pete Punkin.

"Kill them all!" Faggy echoed, gunning down Molero and the Spanish-speaking man.

"Now kill ourselves!" Squeamish shouted, putting the pistol in his mouth and pulling the trigger.

Faggy watched as Squeamish's dead body flopped to the ground beside him.

"That's taking things a bit too far, little buddy," he said quietly.

***

Faggy stood at the end of a dock, smoking a cigarette. He didn't usually smoke, but this occasion seemed to call for a little bit of cancer. A gentle rain sailed down from the clouds, blanketing the earth and Faggy with a feeling of death and release and wetness. In the distance, the seagulls wailed a plaintive eulogy to the lost officers of the 12th Precinct.

Police Chief Sorgum walked up next to Faggy. The two stood in silence, staring into the dark sky and thinking about how hard life is. Finally, Faggy spoke. "Looks like it's gonna rain," he said.

The chief continued staring out to sea, a searching look on his face. "It's already raining, Faggy," the chief answered.

Faggy looked down at the chief, an expression of stone-cold indifference on his face. You can't read Faggy's emotions. Even Faggy can't read Faggy's emotions. But read this loud and clear: if you're on John Faggy's shit list at go time, you best get yourself real gone before he makes you vanish.

Faggy returned his gaze to the sea and shook his head. "You just don't get it, Chief," he said, mostly to himself.

"No, I don't, Faggy," the chief answered quietly. "No, I sure don't."

Faggy flicked his cigarette into the chief's face and walked away down the pier.

He walks, as he stands, triumphalist and alone, intense and focused, a man of the people and the people of a man. Behind his dark glasses lies a world of ultimate complexity and ultimate righteousness. You think you got him pegged? Think again, baby. He knows the way to San Jose, and when he's in San Francisco, he's sure to wear a flower in his hair.

His name is Faggy. John Faggy. And he is one badasssss cracker.

Loving the Monster

by MIKE CIPRA

She bit me only once during the course of our relationship, and I suppose I should be grateful. The bleeding was not nearly as severe as I had anticipated, and her venom took a good ten minutes to travel through my bloodstream. In short, there was more than enough time for me to use my cell phone to call for medical assistance. While relating the details of this embarrassing injury to the emergency operator, I watched my lover at her seat opposite me in the diner, flicking her forked tongue at the remains of my ham-and-cheese omelet. How beautiful she was at that moment, completely indifferent to my suffering!

I will not try to convince you, not for one moment, that I was the victim in this strange love affair. She warned me from the beginning. We were sitting on my apartment's glass balcony, watching the sun set on Los Angeles, and sucking down Tequila-and-raw-egg cocktails.

"I'm trouble," she told me. "Sooner or later, I hurt men who get close to me."

She told me what had happened to the others. A nature photographer named Stephen was in the hospital for a week after he proposed marriage to her during a *National Geographic* shoot. Stephen still wore the scar on his midsection, like a mark of ownership he could not remove. Brent, the handsome but emotionally needy park ranger at Saguaro National Park, had to be flown by helicopter to Arizona State University for antivenin treatment, while Tony, a college kid made overenthusiastic by ecstasy and the pounding beat of a desert rave, had been the most unlucky.

"He wanted to fuck me so much," she said. "It was like his little Maxim-overloaded fraternity brain couldn't fit anything else. I never meant to snuff him, but when he climbed on top of me, talking a lot of gibberish about destiny, trying to force me into something unnatural ... damn, I guess I just blanked out."

"Excuse me. Did you say you killed him?"

"His courting gestures were fucking repulsive. He knew the risks."

"You may be right," I said, "But nobody deserves to die."

"Goddamn it, don't you think I know that?"

We were quiet then. In between our cocktails, the sun had set and the few stars that can be discerned from within the dome of smog that covers Los Angeles had emerged. A minute later, in the lull between an ambulance and a car alarm, I reached over, and tentatively, I touched her. My fingertips traced the mottled patterns of her back, the golden rings that run from her neck down to her tail. She remained motionless. How beautiful she was at that moment, dark and mysterious in the Los Angeles night!

"Gila," I blurted. "I love you."

Had I moved too quickly? Of course I had. But was everything ruined by my impetuous confession?

"Milo," she said. "You're probably the most optimistic motherfucker I've ever met."

She moved in with me immediately, bringing her wonderfully dirty mouth and an odd assortment of habits, but few possessions —literally, three cacti and a blender. In the beginning, Gila rarely slept with me, preferring the crawlspace under the living room couch to the 400-thread-count sheets of my bed. She was fiercely territorial with regard to this niche, hissing and spitting whenever I sat down to watch a basketball game or a news program. I found I had to give up television altogether while I was living with her (and the practice so cleared my head that even now, years later, I rarely watch).

As trust grew between us, Gila shed most of her instinctive hostility, in addition to a layer of dry, scaly skin. Finding pieces of Gila's epidermis on the kitchen floor always made me smile; I took it as a sign that she was becoming comfortable, or at least not quite as self-conscious, around me. Today, I keep scraps of her skin under my bed, in a hard plastic tube meant to store posters.

I would like to think that much of Gila's initial ill humor was a result of having to live in Los Angeles, a city that is many things, but is definitely not *Heloderma suspectum's* natural habitat. Imagine a Gila monster climbing into a Mercedes, trying on a dress at Robinson's-May, or chatting about local politics at a cocktail party. And yet, she performed these tasks with impeccable dignity and remarkable competency.

The whole time, however, I knew she was miserable. The way she talked about the desert, the way she looked east every morning, toward the rising sun and the rugged country where she was hatched, convinced me that her body and her spirit felt the pull of another place.

At this point, I was working seventy-five hours a week for Eaney, Meaney, and Miney, a relatively prestigious Beverly Hills law firm. My life was my career. Although she demanded little else from me, Gila told me she needed more of my time.

"What are those little bald monkey-looking motherfuckers going to do?" Gila asked. "Fire you? Hell no, baby, you're making them money."

Steeled by my love for this beautiful creature, I quickly found the nerve to ask for weekends off. On Friday afternoons then, I would race home from the office to gather up Gila, and we would drive east from Los Angeles, through the dizzying traffic of east-bound freeways, emerging finally into the desert southeast of Joshua Tree National Park. There, the stars would greet our tired eyes and the desert would open its chilly arms in welcome.

Gila could never sleep through the excitement of returning to her native habitat, and, on our first few nights together, she made me a gift of herself—whispering madly, slapping me with her tail, staring with dark eyes. Meteors burned in the sky; the planets jogged slowly around the sun; constellations shimmered; and the movement of these heavenly bodies was reflected in the rhythms of our hallucinatory sex. Undeniably, these strange and passionate nights were the most beautiful of our moments together.

As time went on, however, Gila increasingly abandoned my company, vanishing into the night without a word of excuse or apology. It was as though she heard the desert's singular call, a call I was unable to perceive. Although I never questioned her with regard to these nocturnal adventures (for I was afraid of being too possessive), I can only assume, with a heavy heart, that she was seeking contact with creatures who were more akin to her.

Lizards! While she was away at night, I drank whisky and cursed the desert that had spawned such an unfaithful creature. I cursed myself as well—for being so ugly and ill-conceived that she would desire the company of others. In the final analysis, I was a moderately successful lawyer with a hairy back and a receding hairline. I wanted claws and venom and a beautiful tail like her other lovers. I wanted to live, to find the world's mysterious source for myself, to hear the call that claimed my lover each night, drawing her further from me.

So I got drunk. I stumbled through canyons by moonlight. And, eventually, I wound up passing out under an ocotillo cactus, or next to a boulder of wind-worn granite. Every morning, she would find me. Gila would rouse me with a flick of her forked tongue, and I would be forced to forgive her as noiselessly as she had awakened me. I knew that if I did not get upset, Gila would spend the daylight hours guiding me over sand dunes and through lush gardens of cactus.

No matter the particulars of our daytime exploration or our nightly passions, there was a great deal of sadness in the car on Sunday evening as we hurtled westward via Interstate 10, into the heart of a city I was learning to question. I began to dislike the jarring sensation of pavement against the balls of my feet. I started to resent the burn of smog in my lungs. These things I had not noticed before, and yet, next to the warmth of desert sand or the call of a raven at midday, these impositions seemed obvious.

Despite a growing dissatisfaction with my native city, there was no way I could leave Los Angeles. My livelihood was tied to the practice of law, and my practice of law was tied to a Beverly Hills firm. I could not, at that point, abandon my career.

This conflict between my love life and my professional life came to a head one summer weekend, when I convinced Gila to forsake the usual desert journey in order to attend my firm's annual pool party, at a senior partner's Hollywood Hills mansion.

I tried to find my lover a proper bathing suit, but you can well imagine the difficulties that clothes shopping presented for Gila and myself. After a frustrating morning at the Beverly Center, she ended up going to the party *au naturel*, provoking the scorn of several Westside women, whose bright bikinis and artificial tans gave off an eerie glow in the late afternoon light. Gila grew angry and reticent in their abuse. She retreated to the warmth of the diving board, to sun herself and dream, no doubt, of the desert.

My colleagues pretended to ignore her, out of respect for their wives, but I caught more than one of them gawking at Gila's dark and shapely form. The wives noticed too. I tried to diffuse the growing social tension by means of jokes and small talk, and these tactics proved effective for most of the afternoon. However, when barbecuing began, and I saw Gila saunter over to the grill, I knew that the tenuous peace I had negotiated was about to disintegrate. Oh, my love! You caused quite a sensation, didn't you, flicking your tongue over the entire selection of meat, gulping down a full pound of uncooked wieners before the incredulous crowd.

"Those ignorant motherfuckers hated me anyway," she said as I drove us back to the apartment. "They had already decided that I wasn't worth a shit."

"Why did you have to prove them right?"

"So, you *can* be cruel," she hissed.

"I'm just returning the favor," I answered, with more bile in my voice than I had intended.

She was quiet, and I immediately felt ashamed of my anger.

"Gila, instead of going home, why don't we drive out to the desert? That's where we both feel most comfortable."

"What's the fucking point? We'd just have to come back to this shitty town tomorrow. You're never going to leave your firm, are you? You wouldn't even leave if I asked you to."

"No," I said. "I can't."

The next day she bit me. We went out for breakfast. She ordered six eggs, over easy. Halfway through my hash browns, Gila told me she was leaving.

"I'm going to the desert," she said.

"For how long?"

"For good, Milo."

I told her that she had to stay, that I needed her, that I adored her, that I was unable to leave my job because I did not know how to do anything else. I began crying. I reached out to grab her by the tail, and she bit me then—a deep, justified bite—her lower jaw piercing the skin of my wrist and her glands pumping poison into my wound.

I knew that hitting her would only prolong my pain, so I kept still. I did not call her a monster, even though I was tempted, even though, technically, she was a monster. We simply stared at each other for a few moments, her fangs in my wrist, her poison entering my body, our strange relationship at its zenith, love and jealousy behind us, regret and sadness to follow. It is a strange force indeed that drives us toward any embrace with another creature, when we know in advance how sadly and painfully it must end.

My friends ask me today, why did you stay with that *thing* when all she did was hurt you? Love, I tell them, leaves many questions unanswered, like a veil thrown across sense.

This answer is poetic and very, very insincere. I stayed with Gila because she was more exciting than all of my friends attached to each other and dangled from a golden rope tied to the tallest building in the city. I think often of her, how much she sacrificed by staying in Los Angeles, living in that cramped apartment when the desert lay only ninety miles to the east. How uncomfortable life with me must have been—a long series of impositions, each one more ridiculous and humiliating than the last. Gila, if you could hear me now, I would tell you, again and again, until the words came to my lips like a mantra, I'm sorry.

Fuck literature.

www.contemporarypress.com

Current Titles

Dead Dog by **Mike Segretto**: A curmudgeonly shut-in's life is turned inside-out when he becomes involved with a trash-talking femme fatale, a trio of psychotic gangsters, and a dog whose incessant barking has caused him years of sleepless nights. Spiked with ample doses of sex, violence and campy humor, *Dead Dog* is a riotous road trip from an Arizona trailer park to hell. **ISBN 0-9744614-0-7**

Down Girl by **Jess Dukes**: In *Down Girl*, 29-year-old Pauline Rose Lennon works too hard for every cent she ever made until she meets Anton, willing to give her more cash than she's ever imagined...for one small favor. Pauline's life spins hilariously out of control, but she pulls it back from the brink just in time to prove that just because you're down, it doesn't mean you're out. **ISBN 0-9744614-1-5**

Johnny Astronaut by **Rory Carmichael**: In the future, disco is king. *Johnny Astronaut* is the story of a hard-boiled, hard-drinking P.I. who stumbles upon a mysterious book that changes his life forever. Caught between a vindictive ex-wife, a powerful crime boss, and a sinister race of lizard people, Johnny becomes embroiled in a fast-paced, hilarious adventure that stretches across space and time. **ISBN 0-9744614-3-1**

G.O.P. D.O.A. by **Jay Brida**: While the city braces for 20,000 Republicans to descend on New York, a Brooklyn political operative named Flanagan uncovers a bizarre plot that could trigger a Red, White, Black and Blue nightmare. Populated by buffoons, hacks, thugs and the Sons of Joey Ramone, *G.O.P. D.O.A.* is a fast paced, ripping yarn that gorges on the American buffet of sexual hypocrisy, political ambition and the Republican way of life. **ISBN 0-9744614-5-8**

***How To Smash Everyone To Pieces* by Mike Segretto**: Ex-stunt woman, mass murderer, and champion wise-cracker Mary is furious to discover that her twin sister has been wrangled back to an Arizona prison. Fueled by an unnaturally obsessive love for her twin, Mary sets off on a homicidal cross-country campaign to free Desiree from the clutches of the law. Exploding with action, uproarious one-liners, and more cartoon violence than an episode of *Tom and Jerry*, this is one of the most perverse and hilarious tales ever to come tearing down the highway. **ISBN 0-9744614-6-6**

***Dead Rite* by Jim Gilmore**: Samuel Shelton likes to relax with an ice-cold vodka and a California sunset, but he has a lot on his mind: his wife is dead and his washed up Hollywood starlet of a girlfriend is ignoring him. When Shelton is discovered in a shallow grave, Officer Hicks is on the case. Hicks avoids the media frenzy, and does things by the book until the trail of clues leads straight to putting Hicks at the scene of the crime. Fast-paced and deadly, this is one man's dark trip through the riches of sunny Hollywood. **ISBN 0-9744614-1-5**

Upcoming Titles

I, an Actress by Jeffrey Dinsmore **ISBN 0-9744614-9-0**

The Bride of Trash by Mike Segretto **ISBN 0-9766579-0-2**

Out of body by Tony O'Neill **ISBN 0-9766579-1-0**

contemporary press

Contemporary Press (est. 2003) is committed to truth, justice and going our own way. When Big Publishing dies, we're the cockroaches who will devour their bones and dance on their graves.